KT-561-499

Such Visitors

Such Visitors

Stories by
ANGELA HUTH

HEINEMANN : LONDON

William Heinemann Ltd
Michelin House, 81 Fulham Road, London SW3 6RB

LONDON   MELBOURNE   AUCKLAND

R62538

This collection first published 1989
Copyright © Angela Huth 1989

'The Fuchsia Auberge' originally appeared
in *London Daily News*, 'Ladies' Race' in *Winter's Tales*
and 'Sudden Dancer' in *Woman's Own*.
'The Bull' and 'Irish Coffee' originally
appeared in *Good Housekeeping*. 'Balloons'
originally appeared in *Male and Femail*,
'A Matter of Diplomacy', in *Cosmopolitan*
and 'The Weighing Up' in *Harpers & Queen*.
'Donkey Business', 'Mother of the Bride'
and 'The Weighing Up' have been read
on the BBC's *Morning Story*.

The quotation on p. 141 comes from *The Real Thing* by
Tom Stoppard.
Reproduced by permission of Faber & Faber Ltd.

British Library Cataloguing in Publication Data

Huth, Angela, *1938*–
Such visitors.
I. Title
823'.914[F]

ISBN 0 434 35732 4

Printed and bound by Mackays

For Felicity Binyon

Contents

The Fuchsia Auberge

On the eighth day of the holiday, mid-afternoon in Angers, Anna McGull suffered a crisis no one noticed.

She stood apart from the rest of her family who, for the second time that day, were looking at the famous tapestries. Her husband Michael and her youngest son, Patrick, huddled together, seemed to find as much interest in the guide book as in the tapestries themselves. Simon, the eldest son, stood some distance away, his earnest stare fixed upon the Apocalypse. When contemplating any work of art, Simon managed to exude an air of superiority, as if he alone were granted understanding. His father and brother, a little awed by this attitude, believed Simon had a vision they lacked: hence their endless perusal of guide books to make up in facts what they lacked in spiritual communication. Anna had no such feelings. Simon's loftiness drove her wild. She thought he looked quite goofy, peering through his thick spectacles, fingers twitching at his sludge-coloured anorak. For years, she had struggled to fight the annoyance his physical presence caused her. It had never been so bad as on this holiday.

Outside, it gently rained. A flat, plum-coloured light in the galleries darkened the tapestries. Anna wondered if any of the women who had put thousands of hours of work into these hangings of gloomy beauty had ever rebelled. The younger ones, surely, must have woken some mornings and thought to themselves they would go mad if they had to do another bloody stitch.

Anna's reflections were cut short by a Norwegian tourist. He stepped in front of her, blocking her view and provoking the crisis. His mackintosh skimmed calves latticed with veins: bare toes splayed beyond the edges of his sandals, clenched in

3

concentration. Anna thought: in the past week I've seen forty-three Romanesque churches, fifteen museums, eleven châteaux, seven picture galleries, the tapestries *twice* . . . and now a Norwegian is thwarting my view. I can't bear it any more.

She left the gallery, hurried outside. It was raining harder, now. Sheltering under a chestnut tree, she looked up into the great dome of sharp green leaves and thanked God there was nothing in the guide book about *this*. The very thought of the guide book made her cry for a moment. Soon she would recover herself, return to the gallery, wait.

But as she was dabbing her eyes an English couple walked by. Plainly happy, the man took the woman's arm and guided her towards a café. His innocent gesture caused Anna a second crisis, this time of jealousy. Michael and the boys would never consider stopping mid-afternoon for a drink. Three more churches before dark, they would say.

Anna followed the couple into the café. She chose an empty table by the window, ordered a croissant and coffee. (Lunch had been a bag of apples eaten beside an ancient tomb.) Her aching legs and feet recovered. The pleasure of sitting alone at a foreign table uncluttered by guide books was almost tangible.

After a while she saw her husband and sons leave the gallery. They looked briefly about them, then set off towards the church. The English couple rose to leave.

'Where are you going?' Anna heard herself asking.

'Delange, ten miles north. We've been staying in an auberge there, but we've got to get back to Paris.'

The woman smiled, friendly. Then Anna heard herself requesting a lift.

They sped along a small road that followed a curling river. Silver birches shimmered high above white cows, and higher still white clouds feathered the sky. What am I doing? Anna thought, just once.

The auberge was the sort of place she had been hoping to find ever since landing in France. In her mind a fuchsia auberge (baskets of flowers hanging round the terrace) represented warmth, peace, an hour or two to herself. Michael and the boys, of course, were not interested in such things. Convenience for the sights was all they cared about. Station hotels. But she was alone now. She could do as she liked. Anna

4

quickly decided the place was much too agreeable to leave within the hour. Besides, there was no transport. She booked in for the night.

Her room had blue-striped walls, curtains dizzy with flowers, a freckled mirror in a heavy frame. The window looked on to a narrow garden of apple trees and lupins. A grey cat, ears laid back, snaked across the grass and jumped up on to a wall. Small gusts of windy rain, splattering against the window, were the only cracks in the silence.

So this is freedom, Anna thought, and put out her hand to touch it: the silky bed cover, the cold brass of the bedstead. She climbed under the eiderdown and with no feelings of disloyalty reflected what a relief it was to be in a *silent* bed: no Michael beside her rumbling on about tomorrow's plans or today's churches. Then she fell asleep.

It was almost dark when she woke. Away from the family for four hours . . . Guilt brushed her lightly. Much stronger was a kind of nefarious excitement, a feeling of adventure. The word caused her to smile to herself with a touch of scorn. If an afternoon's sleep in a French auberge was an adventure, how dull was the rest of her life?

Downstairs in the salon – open fire, smell of lavender – the guilt vanished altogether. Half a dozen couples – here for the fishing, she supposed – all seemed to be drinking champagne. The place reminded her of a small hotel in Galway where she and Michael had spent a last holiday alone before the children were born. They would sit on the bank of the river all day, Michael tweaking at his rod, she reading *War and Peace*. After a dinner of grilled fish they would play Scrabble by the fire, and have a glass of Irish whiskey before bed. That had been a good holiday, long ago.

Michael, these days, hated spending money on frivolous drinks. In private defiance, Anna ordered herself a glass of champagne. Careless of her light head, she chose a seat and drank fast. Then, rising cautiously, she went to the telephone and rang the hotel in Angers.

Michael and the boys were out.

'*Sortis pour le dîner*,' the receptionist said.

Anna was silenced for a moment. Loyalty and compassion

5

had forced her to make this call. She had imagined them worried, searching.

'Were they looking for me?' she asked at once.

'*Absolument pas.*'

'Please say I'll be back tomorrow.'

Returning to the bar, annoyed by her burning cheeks, Anna found a full glass of champagne on her table. Puzzled, she caught the eye of a man she had noticed before. He sat alone.

'*Je vous en prie, Madame,*' he said quietly, and lowered his head into his newspaper before Anna, in her confusion, could thank him.

Her hand now trembled on the glass. The extraordinary gesture had blasted all thoughts of her family from her mind. She felt the warmth of vanity. Her profile, she remembered, had always been good. Perhaps the remnants of other attractions were still recognisable. After a while she allowed herself to glance at the sender of the champagne. Nice face, hair drooping endearingly over one eye.

Suddenly, the way things were going became marvellously clear to her. She thanked God for the double bed, though how would she manage without a dressing-gown? The man raised his eyes.

They looked at each other searingly, recognising their mutual intent. Anna got up, left the salon. She would go straight to her room, rip off her clothes and let the stranger begin.

Somehow she found herself guided by the friendly proprietor to the dining-room. A candle burned on her corner table, a vase of blue lupins made pearly shadows on the white cloth. She ordered dinner. Passion would have to be postponed for an hour or so. Soon the man would follow, make his next move.

As she sipped at the stranger's champagne, Anna found herself wondering at her cold-blooded lack of guilt as she contemplated imminent infidelity. After twenty-three years of absolute faithfulness, here she was suddenly confronted by the prospect of adultery, determined to break every rule she had ever lived by, to behave like a whore. She shivered, enthralled at the thought.

She was halfway through her wild duck when the man

eventually entered the dining-room accompanied by a girl of about twelve – plainly his daughter. He gave Anna a brief smile full of purpose, then sat with his back to her and started a conversation with the child. Pity, considering the scarcity of time, Anna thought. But there was also something luxurious about *not* being able to have dinner with him.

By ten o'clock she was naked in bed, waiting. The sound of voices and the banging of cooking pots came from downstairs. Two hours went by. Footsteps creaked outside her room. Doors shut. Silence.

Tense with anticipation, Anna found herself wondering if just one night with a stranger would do anything to jeopardise twenty-three solid years of marriage. Might the placing of one foot on the slippery slope mean a general descent? Would it whet a long-dormant appetite, underline her discontent? It was hard to judge in advance. The self is so surprising. Maybe, from now on, she would break out in all sorts of directions. Maybe she would start to acknowledge the looks that Jack, Michael's oldest friend, had been giving her for years. Maybe she would become impervious to the boys' lack of consideration and, with other things on her mind, be irritated by them no longer. Maybe she would spend some money on herself, for once: resuscitate her rusty smile . . . cut and redden her hair, go off to London on Michael's nights out at the Round Table, the Parish Council, the Rock Gardeners' Club, and the Regiment's endless reunions . . .

The silence continued. Anna lay awake all night. The man did not come. The cold she felt became the cold of foolishness and shame. Desolate, she dressed at dawn, stood for a long time at the window watching a hard sun rise over the lupins. Escape had been quite spoiled by her own stupidity, her own crushed vanity. Also, she must now query her own judgement. How could she have been so wrong about the man's intentions?

By eight, she was downstairs settling the bill. Through stinging eyes, she observed a mistake. She had been charged for two glasses of champagne.

'A gentleman paid for one,' she explained.

'Apologies,' said the proprietor at once. 'Of course: Monsieur Cadeau. He gave instructions. Whenever he's here he

7

buys everyone in the place a glass of champagne. Good for – how do you say? Public relations.'

Anna felt the blood scour her face.

'Who is Monsieur Cadeau?' she asked.

The proprietor's smile indicated it was not the first time he had had to solve this puzzle.

'He works for a champagne firm,' he said.

A taxi took Anna back to Angers. At the hotel she found Michael and the boys at breakfast. They showed no surprise at her return.

'Had fun?' asked Michael. 'You might have left a proper message. Still, we didn't worry. We knew you wouldn't do anything silly.'

The boys, engrossed in guide books, asked no questions.

'Delange is the plan for today,' Michael went on. 'Looks like an interesting church.' He turned almost contrite eyes to his wife. 'I see it has a pretentious auberge, your sort of thing. Would you like – ?'

'Oh no,' said Anna quickly. 'I went there. You wouldn't like it at all.'

From a long way off, she registered Michael's relief, and her sons' clumsy hands thrashing about among their guide books and maps, eager to be off.

'Buck up with your coffee, Mum,' said Simon.

Was there anything more bleak than return from a flight that had failed?

In the car, Michael said, 'Let's take the small road, follow the river.'

I could always try again, thought Anna.

'Did you look at the church?' asked Simon, zipping up his horrible anorak.

'No,' said Anna. 'I didn't go there to see the church.'

Turning her attention to the map, she found the road that led to Monsieur Cadeau of the champagne firm.

'On our way then,' said Michael.

But I don't suppose I will, thought Anna.

En famille once more, the McGulls then set off for the ninth day of their sightseeing tour of France.

Mother of the Bride

*A*fter much deliberation Mrs Hetherington decided against taking any tranquillisers. Better, she thought, to witness the whole thing with a clear mind than through an unreal calm induced by pills. If a tear should come to her eye – why, that was the prerogative of every bride's mother. Few people would see and those who did might understand.

When she had taken her decision Mrs Hetherington had not envisaged the strength of emotion that would affect her on the Big Day. So it was with some surprise, here and now in the church, the journey up the aisle having been accomplished with dignity on the arm of her brother John, that she felt frills of sweat at the back of her knees. And her hands, stuffed into navy gloves one size too small, trembled in disconcerting fashion.

She had chosen to wear navy with the thought that it was the most appropriate colour for her particular role at the wedding. Nobody could accuse her of trying to steal the bride's thunder – as did so many mothers, perhaps unconsciously – and yet, if they observed her closely, Mrs Hetherington's friends would see that her clothes conveyed the quiet chic she had always managed to achieve. She had chosen them with care: silk dress, matching coat, straw hat bearing the only small flourish of which she could be accused – an old-fashioned rose on its moiré band. On a November morning of early snow she had taken shelter in Debenhams and come upon the whole outfit, piece by lucky piece: even bag, shoes and gloves. In the small changing-room she had examined her appearance with the sort of critical eye no bride's mother can afford to be without. How would it all look five months hence under a blue April sky? Mrs Hetherington would have liked to have asked Alice's opinion – after all, it was by tradition supposed to be

11

Alice's day – but her daughter was off on a 'holiday' raising funds for overseas famine relief. She was funny like that, Alice. No interest in appearance – never had had. It had been all Mrs Hetherington could do to persuade her daughter in March – cutting it pretty tight – to concentrate on her own wedding dress. No: Alice had never so much as asked her mother what *she* was going to wear, and in all the flurry of getting ready it was unlikely she had noticed. Or cared.

Precisely what Alice did care for, Mrs Hetherington was sometimes at a loss to know. As a child she had been straightforward enough – ordinary, really, except for her freckles. A fondness for rabbits rather than ponies; some talent at the high jump, which petered out at puberty; an inclination towards history, which petered out after 'O' levels; and no traumas that Mrs Hetherington could recall. Except perhaps for the time Alice had thrown scrambled egg at her father on the last morning of their holiday at Brancaster, calling him a fuddy-duddy (and worse) for not allowing her to stay at the village disco later than midnight. But that had been an exceptional time, and David had made his point clumsily, Mrs Hetherington had to agree. She put the incident down to teenage wilfulness and considered herself lucky she had such a comparatively easy offspring.

It was only when she thought about it later that it occurred to her that Alice's 'distance', as she called it, dated from that holiday. This 'distance' itself was so hard to define that Mrs Hetherington refrained from mentioning it even to David, lest he should consider her ridiculous. But to Mrs Hetherington, who could never be accused of insensitivity, the widening gap between their daughter and her parents seemed noticeably to develop. It wasn't that Alice changed in any outward way: she remained the polite, willing, quiet creature she had always been, dutiful to her parents and apparently content to come home most weekends. But of her weekday life in London Mrs Hetherington was aware she knew nothing beyond the facts: Alice had a research job in television – exactly what that meant Mrs Hetherington had always been a little unclear and never remembered, somehow, to ask. She shared a flat with an old school friend in Shepherd's Bush: not a very salubrious part of London, but still. What she got up to in the evenings Mrs

Hetherington had no idea, though several times when she had rung after nine at night Alice had been in, giving rise to the comfortable thought that at least her daughter spent many evenings at home watching television. Once, when Mrs Hetherington had conversationally mentioned a demonstration in Trafalgar Square that had been given much attention in the papers, Alice casually remarked that she had been there and it wasn't half as bad as the publicity made out. Well, thought Mrs Hetherington at the time, Alice must have been passing. She had never been a *political* girl, that was for sure. She could happily have bet her bottom dollar Alice would have no interest in the terrible carryings-on of the National Front, or those dreadful Militants.

As for men in her daughter's life – Mrs Hetherington's speculations flailed about in a total void. No evidence of any kind to go on. Some weekends Alice would stare into the distance, sandy eyelashes (from David) fluttering thoughtfully, and make a point of answering the telephone first. When the call was for her she would speak in a low, unrecognisable voice: hard to hear from the other side of the door where Mrs Hetherington would hover – not out of curiosity, of course, but from natural anxiety about what was going on. If Alice had any boyfriends she never brought them home. Mrs Hetherington could not understand why. She had always made it clear she was eager to entertain any of Alice's friends. 'Do bring whoever you like to stay, darling,' she would say every Sunday evening Alice was at home. But Alice would always reply she preferred her weekends alone.

Then, out of the blue, no warning, there had been the event of Alastair. Mrs Hetherington would never forget it. Glancing at the stained-glass windows above the altar, whose unkind colours recharged the tears in her eyes, she remembered the occasion once again. Alice had not acted in the most thoughtful way, it had to be admitted. Not a warning telephone call, even. Just, that Friday evening, arriving with him.

'Thought you wouldn't mind, Mum,' she said, 'if I brought Alastair Mead. We're going to get married.'

David, bless him, had taken it very well. Fetched the last bottle of Krug from the cellar and was talking easily to Mr Mead, about mortgages, within moments. (Mr Mead, it

13

seemed, was something to do with mortgages 'for the bread and butter', Alice said. In his spare time, his real vocation, he raised money for famine relief.) Their conversation gave Mrs Hetherington time to study her future son-in-law: she saw a shortish, chunky figure, head slightly too big for his body, the loose smile of lips not quite in control, falling socks. She sipped rapidly at her drink to conceal her disappointment. In her heart of hearts she had always hoped her son-in-law would cut something of a dash: the brutal truth about Mr Mead was that he would not turn a head in the most plebeian crowd. Still, he had been to Charterhouse, as he let drop with his second glass of champagne, and perhaps his charm lay in his mind. He must be given a fair chance, Mrs Hetherington told herself, and in time Alice might wean him off tweed ties. Dreadful to be so prejudiced by appearances, but Mrs Hetherington had always been like that. It was unfair that a stranger's cast of nose or choice of shoe could breed in her such instant prejudice, but there it was. Suddenly Mrs Hetherington knew that she hated Alastair Mead, both for himself and for his proprietory talk about Alice. But she smiled bravely, and no one could have guessed her feelings.

Next morning the two of them appeared at breakfast blatantly haggard. Well, Mrs Hetherington and David had done a bit of passage-creeping in their time, but at least they had had the decency to disguise the effects of their naïve kisses next morning. With a shudder Mrs Hetherington handed Alastair a kipper. He should have known better than to lay hands on Alice the first night under her parents' roof. Also, he had cut himself shaving and a thread of blood looped down his chin to join a clot of dried toothpaste in the corner of his mouth. All distasteful to her, poor man. In twenty-nine years David had never cut himself shaving: it wasn't necessary. As for Alice, she could have combed her hair, surely, and done something to conceal her satiated state. It wasn't that Mrs Hetherington disapproved of sex before marriage, naturally: everyone did it these days and Alice, she had no doubt, had relinquished her virginity some years ago. But up to now she had had the tact to protect her mother from evidence of her affairs. Would that she had not let matters slip just because she had an engagement ring – and a very minor pearl, at that – on her finger.

14

Mrs Hetherington's thoughts were only interrupted by Alastair's irritating pecking at his kipper, and his boring remembrances of childhood kippers in Scotland, implying criticism of the Macfisheries' pedigree of the present fish. In all, Mrs Hetherington found the whole weekend a trial. She could not deny the probity of Alastair's character, but kept furiously to herself the disappointment at his lack of humour and style. Worst of all, he supported Alice in her desire for a quick register office wedding. But on that point Mrs Hetherington was adamant, unbudgeable. It was to be a white wedding with all the trimmings, for her sake if not for theirs.

The organ played Bach, swelling to greet Mrs Hetherington's present feeling of satisfaction as she reflected on her efforts in the past months. She had tried, and she had triumphed. There was genuine love in her heart, now, for her son-in-law. Even admiration. The way he worked such long hours in his mortgage business and then gave up his weekends to famine relief. His solid principles: only live in the way you can afford (they were to start off in a small rented house in Twickenham) and put work before pleasure. He had planned with touching care a honeymoon trip around Inverness. Mrs Hetherington wouldn't have cared for any such thing herself, of course: she and David had cruised to Panama. However, Alice seemed happy in general. And, in trying to see Alastair through her daughter's eyes, Mrs Hetherington had almost certainly succeeded in discovering his charm – if devotion counts as a charm. She found it hard to forgive his dandruff and his anorak, a particularly nasty blue – but they were unimportant externals, weren't they? It was his character that counted and, by God, by now, she loved that. She really did. The love had been flamed by others' approval: his prospects, his solidity, his charity. But no matter how it had been come by, it was there. The real love of Mrs Hetherington for her son-in-law Alastair Mead.

She glanced at the gold watch embedded in her wrist. Only a minute to go. Very moving, the music, whatever it was. Half an hour ago she had witnessed the poignant sight of Alice struggling into her white satin. She looked – cliché or not – radiant. Alastair was a very lucky man. Mrs Hetherington let her eyes fall upon his back view. He had had a haircut, it

15

seemed. And he looked a little taller in his morning suit. Rather endearing, the way he kept nervously whispering to the best man. Of course – and this was a wicked and secret thought – in Mrs Hetherington's experience of weddings, Etonians undoubtedly made the least nervous bridegrooms. She'd noticed that over the years. (David, in the Guards Chapel, had been wonderfully untrembling, giving her courage.) But given the less noble training of Charterhouse, Alastair wasn't doing too badly so far. Straight shoulders, almost as if he'd been in the army. Mrs Hetherington wished her brother, who was still in the army, could contain his asthmatic wheezing, irritating at such a solemn time. Still, the marguerite trees at the altar had been an inspiration. (Hers.) Oh dear God, where were they? A minute late and her left shoe was hurting.

She heard the hush that precedes a bride's entrance. With a supreme effort of will Mrs Hetherington remained facing the altar. Alastair, weaker, turned. His face was pale, the jowls loosened by trepidation. Dear Alastair. Would he were just a few inches . . . But all right so long as Alice never wore stilettos. Had David ordered enough champagne? And Alice's heart: was it beating like her own? Funny how such disparate thoughts topple over one another at such moments. What on earth could they be *doing*? Darling Alice, such a loving daughter.

Glorious things of Thee are spoken . . .

Ah, they must be on their way at last. Oh my Alice . . . the way she laughed in the bath so much at two; and how she cried that time she fell off her bicycle into the shrubbery at four. And all those things she had made at school: painted fir-cones and potato-cut calendars. No better presents in the whole world, were there? Impossible to think of her as a married woman. Oh dear, they must be halfway up the aisle by now. Well at least Alice wouldn't be in fearful anticipation of It, as Mrs Hetherington herself had been. Rather a shame, really, that particular excitement already over. But it was awful to be thinking of her own daughter in such terms at all, wasn't it? And here she was at last, misty faced under her veil. Pity about no posy of gardenias, as Mrs Hetherington would have liked, but Alice had insisted on the austerity of a prayer book. Anyway, she was beautiful. Well, almost. David's handsome

16

bones were a bit strong on a girl, perhaps: it had to be said Alice's face was not one of infinite delicacy. But today it was at its best, all for Alastair Mead.

'Let us pray,' said the vicar.

Navy patent bow dug less into her foot now she was on her knees. Thank God. Thank God for having given her a daughter like Alice. That time she had been so homesick at her finishing school in Paris – oh God forgive me for all my inadequacies as a mother. Darling Alice forgive me too and try to be happy. Try to keep those promises like Daddy and I have done. It may be awfully boring sometimes, but it's worth trying. And don't desert us. Why didn't I put my handkerchief up my sleeve instead of in my bag – it would make too much noise, opening it. Mustn't sniff . . . Come home whenever you want to and bring your friends. And I promise to be a good grandmother. Baby-sit at any time. Oh you were such an adorable baby, and so good. Mrs Alastair Mead. Well, who on earth would want their daughter to marry a flashy duke? Who'd really want their daughter to be a sudden duchess?

They were in their seats, now, listening to the address. It was a little hard to hear, even here in the front row: something about the importance of putting someone else *first*, for the rest of your life. Very moving. Pity those further back wouldn't be able to hear the message. But then the servants of God were inclined to mumble too humbly. Putting Alastair Mead *first*: what a thought. Who on earth could want . . . ? Mrs Hetherington glanced at her husband, firm beside her, slight smile. Dear David: his handsome rugged face, the calm of a good colonel in all crises. Though naturally this wasn't a crisis, was it? But a very happy day.

There was much kissing in-between signing the register. Alastair's cheek was damp with nervous sweat. He smelt of the worst kind of after-shave. Alice glowed at him, brown mascara clotting her eyelashes. No words: what could Mrs Hetherington say? Thank goodness this part of it was nearly over. Called upon to be efficient at the reception, her role would come more easily. It was all this hovering about, second lead to the star, that caused the strain. Stiffly she followed David back to their pew, eyes down, aware of the blur of

17

wedding hats and curious faces. Mean thought: mostly *their* friends. The Meads' side was half empty . . .

Optimistic blast of the organ. Finale. Darling Alice. As she appeared on Alastair's arm Mrs Hetherington briefly shut her eyes to protect the scalding balls. On opening them she felt them lashed with tears in spite of all the self-control. Perhaps she should have taken a pill after all.

Alice smiling, now. Alastair smiling. Stupid flaccid smile of triumph at his catch. For after all, Alice *was* something of a catch. Sparkle of dandruff on his shoulder. Wedding socks no doubt wrinkled. God forgive her, but Mrs Hetherington couldn't love him any more. Her first instincts had been right. Nothing could alter the fact that he was a humourless dreary prig: there was not a single thing about him over which she could rejoice.

Still, sons-in-law are sent to try us, and she would battle on. She stepped into the aisle, let Alastair's dreadful father, pink-eyed, take her arm. She gave a wonderful smile to the congregation at large, acknowledging the happiness of the day. And with eyes never leaving the distant white cloud that was her beloved daughter, refusing to limp in spite of the agony of her shoe, she made the kind of irreproachable journey down the aisle which can only cause the wedding guests to observe: what a perfect mother of the bride.

Ladies' Race

On the third anniversary of the death of their friend, the chief mourners, perhaps the only mourners left, visited the graveyard with their customary bunch of daffodils. They wore black coats, signifying the formality that had insinuated itself into their lives – a thing they were both aware of, fought against, but seemed unable to change. The man, hands crossed, wore bright new leather gloves. The woman's hands, also crossed, were bare: the nails bitten away, flaky, lustreless. They remained in uneasy silence for some moments, heads bowed, eyes on the simple headstone that was engraved with the two names of their friend, the date of her birth and the date of her death.

The man shifted. Relieved, the woman took his arm. She regarded this annual gesture of respect as pointless. Surely they should forget, not remember. But Gerald was insistent, and she had learned not to cross him on important matters. All the same, she could not resist observing how she felt: Gerald should know.

'Anyone would think this was the most important anniversary of the year, to you,' she said.

Gerald made no reply. They turned towards the path of pale sharp stones that ran stiffly between the graves. Leaning against each other, like people older than their years, they began to walk towards the gate. It was cold, in spite of the thickness of their coats. But, heavy with marriage, it was no time to hurry. These visits always bared their memories, troubled them for a few hours, or days, or even weeks.

Gerald met Lola first. She was tall, head above most women at the party. It was a cold house, and while others gathered shawls about their shoulders Lola was impressive for her long

21

bare arms and the warm-looking flesh of her neck and half-exposed bosom. Gerald, who had had no lover for two years, partly for the good of his soul but mostly for the lack of suitable women, found himself inclining towards her. As he fetched her a glass of wine and another plate of haddock kedgeree – her third – he considered the possibility of breaking his vow of self-inflicted chastity. The thought was an unformed, uncoloured thing: the merest web that flung itself across his tired mind. But registered. Meantime, as a patient man, he was surprised to find himself annoyed by the queue at the buffet. He had left Lola alone in a corner and could see a gathering tide of men beginning to converge upon her.

But she greeted him on his return with the kind of quiet pleasure that evaporated her new admirers. Not that she had much to say to Gerald. She seemed quite content to sit silently by him, wolfing her kedgeree, apparently hungry. Gerald, dry with weariness from weeks of over-work, was grateful for her lack of demand: he was in no mood to bewitch, or even entertain. He felt at ease in her silence, and grateful for it.

Much later they walked down the frosty street to his car. Lola wore no coat, said she never felt cold. Gerald was briefly shot with the desire to feel her flesh, to prove her boastful warmth. Instead he put his hands in his pockets and kept his distance. The filmy stuff of her dress blew about as she walked, making her seem fragile, for all her height. In the seat of his old sports car she had to bunch up her long legs: Gerald found himself apologising. Sarah – what years ago *she* suddenly seemed – had always managed to stretch out her minuscule limbs with great comfort. Lola laughed, easing the nervousness Gerald always felt when a new woman entered the sanctity of his car. She lived, it turned out, quite near him.

Some days later, by the gas fire in his muddled sitting-room, Gerald discovered his first impression of Lola had been quite wrong. There was nothing frail about her. No: she was an athletic girl with calves of lively muscle and wrist bones that were handsome in their size. While she ate her way through his last supplies of Dundee cake and shortbread, she told him something of her outdoor life: she had played tennis one year at Junior Wimbledon; she skied each winter, sailed every summer, rode at weekends, jogged round Hyde Park three

22

mornings a week before breakfast – hated her secret job at the Foreign Office. Gerald was momentarily alarmed by the thought of such outdoor energy: worlds that were far from his. But then she smiled, brushing crumbs from her chin with the back of her hand, and he felt relieved again.

'I suppose you think just because of all that I'm very hearty, don't you?' she said. 'I learned judo till I was fourteen and I could fling my older brother over my shoulder, easy as anything.' Her eyes sparkled over Gerald's weary body, hunched deep in his armchair. 'As a matter of fact, I expect I could still . . .'

Gerald shifted. 'I'm sure you could,' he said.

'Shall I try?'

She was both mischievous and serious. Gerald was torn between not wanting to disappoint her, and wishing to preserve some dignity.

'Is this quite the place?' he asked, glancing about the piles of books.

'Oh, anywhere'll do, won't it?'

Lola was already up, enormous above him, smiling her enchanting smile as she pulled him to his feet. He sensed scaling up the side of her as if in a fast lift: flat stomach, mounds of bosom beneath wool, thin neck, pretty teeth. Just for a second his eyes were level with hers. Then, the crash. He was grovelling on his own Turkish carpet, the small square of ugly reds and blues that for years he had meant to change, and had never been forced to study so closely before. He heard the sound of falling books, felt pain in elbows and knees. Lola was laughing, helping him up again.

'There . . . Honestly. I told you. You all right?'

'Fine.' Gerald had cupped his face in one hand, was pulling at the blue skin beneath his eyes. 'You're still very good,' he said.

'Well, it's nice to know I can still do it. Self-defence is very important these days. Of course, you aren't that heavy.' Gerald returned to his chair to hide his affront. 'And I was scarcely attacking you.'

'No. But you might have been. Anyhow, you were very sporting.'

'Thanks.'

23

Lola bent down and kissed him quickly on the temple. One bosom rubbed his nose. Her jersey smelt slightly of mixed herbs. He watched her, in her kneeling position on the ground again, pour more tea and finish the cake.

'You should meet my friend Rose,' she said. 'She's the real one for judo. Though you'd never guess her strength, just looking at her. She's half my size.'

By the time Lola left it was almost dark. She claimed she had to be somewhere far away by six, and must hurry. From his first-floor window Gerald watched her run down the front path. She left large foot-prints in the new snow – it must have fallen during the afternoon. Funny they hadn't noticed it. Rubbing his elbow, Gerald wondered where she was going. He turned back to the fallen piles of books. Attempting to restore some order, he tried not to think. The evening ahead seemed long and empty. The warmth of the room, always to be relied on, had gone with Lola. The thief, he thought. The impudent thief. He wouldn't let her go, next time.

There followed a week of absence. Lola was away on some secret mission. But she rang, as promised, on her return – within half an hour of her return, as a matter of fact, Gerald noticed. She asked him to supper next evening. Just a stew, she said, and Rose might drop in.

Gerald spent a day of happy anticipation, enjoying the patience that comes with knowing there are only a few hours to pass. He tried to get used to the strange sensation that in time he and Lola might become proper friends. He bought two expensive bottles of wine, one white, one red, and rather hoped Lola would be alone.

But Rose was already there, peeling potatoes, exuding an air of efficiency that Lola altogether lacked. She was small and curvaceous, with pale wavy hair that kept falling about her face, changing its shape from moment to moment. She had vast yellow-green eyes that slanted cat-like, and one dimple when she smiled. The warmth of her was so powerful that for a moment Gerald saw Lola as a cold and distant mountain. Then the mountain laughed in absolute delight at his extravagant wine, and his lonely week without her turned to dust.

Over dinner in the small, hard kitchen with its dreadful

24

strip lighting and vegetable-patterned curtains, Gerald learned that Rose and Lola were childhood friends. They had been brought up together in Dorset, gone to school together, shared a love of sport and (much laughter in recalling the incidents) even a boyfriend in their teens. They still met at least once a week and, Gerald supposed, confided to each other the intimate secrets of their hearts in that peculiar way that girls seem unable to resist. They spoke of their sporting life, of course, praising each other's qualities of stamina and speed.

'Rose can run miles and *miles* without getting out of breath,' explained Lola. 'She always won the cross-country at school. There was no one to touch her.'

'Ah, but Lola's high jump,' declared Rose. '*That* was something. She broke all records.'

Gerald enjoyed the evening. The girls, chattering on almost as if he was not there, made him relax and smile. Having drunk most of the excellent wine himself, and having been persuaded to eat far too much of the heavy stew, a delightful sleepiness came upon him. Lola and Rose, immersed in their memories, didn't seem to notice his drooping eyelids. He could watch them unobserved. With some incredulity he reflected how only ten days ago there was no woman in his life with whom he could have wanted to spend the evening. Now here he was enjoying himself with two new ones, relishing their quite different attractions, and their friendliness. It was not the night, however – as during the afternoon he had vaguely thought it might be – to lay a gentle hand on Lola. For some reason, he would not want Rose to know any such thoughts had crossed his mind. And were he not to leave before Lola, Rose would be bound to guess his intentions.

So he left early, mumbling about an early start next morning. The girls were dismayed, but understanding. They both kissed him warmly on the cheek.

In his chilly bed, two hours later, Gerald was still thinking about them: Rose's eyes, Lola's smile; Rose's waist, Lola's full bosom. Both had rippling laughs, soft voices. Forced to choose between them, though, Lola would be his. She had a rare quality of calm, for all her mischievous fun, that gave him strength. Besides that, she was a creature of extraordinary

25

sensitivity: in the laughing discussion they had had about judo she had given Gerald a look but made no mention of the event that proved her skills had not rusted. Gerald would always be grateful to her for that. Lola, Lola, Lola, he said to himself: it's a cold night without you.

Then he heard the ring of his front door bell. He hurried downstairs, puzzled. He was not a man on whom unannounced visitors eagerly called. Something must be wrong. Gerald felt the excitement of fear.

Rose, muffled in a fur coat, stood on his doorstep. She held out his grey wool scarf.

'You left this behind . . . Sorry. Have I woken you? Thought I'd drop it in as I was passing.'

'Good heavens. No. Yes. I mean, well – look, do come in. Afraid I'm in my pyjamas.'

'Are you sure?' Rose was already in the hall, snowflakes on the fur glinting in the dim light.

"Course. We'll have some whisky.'

He put on his dressing-gown, she kept on her coat. They sat on the floor by the gas fire, listening to its quiet buzz, aware of the full moon through the window.

'Sorry it's so cold,' said Gerald. 'I keep meaning to put in central heating, but can't face all the palaver.'

'That's all right.' Rose shivered and smiled. 'That was the most heavenly evening, wasn't it? I can't think why, but I know I'll remember it as a particularly nice evening. Won't you?'

'Yes,' said Gerald. 'Think I probably will.'

'Lola says you've only met twice.'

'That's right.'

'She's the best person, actually, I've ever met.'

'Ah,' said Gerald. 'I can see she seems a . . . good sort.'

Rose laughed. 'What do you mean, a good sort? I've never heard anything so pompous.'

In the fraction of the second that her eyes were closed with laughter, Gerald flung himself awkwardly against her, pushing her flat on to the floor. He kissed her with all the hunger that had been pent within him, festering, for two years. She wriggled furrily beneath him, murmuring something about knowing the moment she saw him it would end like this.

26

'But can't we go somewhere more comfortable?' she said.

They spent the night in Gerald's bed.

Rose stayed three nights and three days. During that time she tidied Gerald's flat, changed the sheets and bath towels, brightened the place with Christmas roses and winter leaves. Gerald would come back in the evening and find her cooking casseroles that smelt of past holidays in the South of France, a butcher's apron belted tightly round her tiny waist. Each evening he found himself unable to wait for the pleasure of her until after dinner, and later at night he would fall deeply asleep in her arms.

On the fourth morning she announced she had better be getting back to her flat. Gerald, whose reasoning was never its liveliest at breakfast, struggled with himself. He reflected on the speed with which a man can turn from solitude to cohabitation, and with what ease the new state of living together can feel like an old habit. He thought of asking her to stay, to live with him for a while. But she had already packed the small case she had fetched from her flat. She was washing the breakfast things with an air of finality. An invitation to stay, at that moment, would have seemed presumptuous. So Gerald let her go, all smiles and thanks for the happy time, anticipating a welcome return to his solitary state.

But when he got back to the flat that evening, still smelling slightly of Rose's scent, the breakfast things where she had left them tidily on the table, aloneness seemed less desirable.

He lit the fire, whose hiss had become confoundedly nostalgic, and a small cigar. He poured himself a drink and tried to concentrate on his briefs for the complicated case next day. But there was no heart in his concentration, no appetite for the cold food Rose had thoughtfully left in the fridge. Damn the girl. He found himself humming a tune from a musical of twenty years ago. At the age he had seen it the words had held no meaning for him: *I was serenely independent/And content before we met . . .*

And he would be again, given a few days. It was not as if he had wanted her, or any woman, to insinuate herself into his well-structured life. In so many years of bachelordom he had

27

learned the art of subtle evasion and self-protection. Rose had merely stirred some superficial desire in him, vulnerable after two years' chastity.

All the same, by nine o'clock he decided to ring her and tell her to come back. Just to talk. As he moved to the telephone, hesistant in the knowledge of his weakness, it rang. Rose, then, was even weaker than he: Gerald was glad.

'For Christ's sake, come back quickly,' he said, no time to think of more reticent words.

'Come back? It's Lola, not Rose.'

'Lola? I'm sorry. How nice.' He had almost forgotten her in the last few days.

'Rose has had to go home to Yorkshire to nurse her mother who's dying of cancer.'

'Oh. I'm sorry. I wonder she didn't tell me herself.'

'She thought about it, but decided the news would be inappropriate during the last few days.'

Gerald silently marvelled at Rose's sensitivity.

'It might have made a difference,' he agreed.

'I mean, one doesn't want to burden new friends with serious problems, does one?' There was remarkable lightness in Lola's voice.

'No, of course not. Look here . . . What are you doing? Why don't you come round for a drink?'

The invitation was a reflex action. Having heard himself make the fatal suggestion, Gerald suddenly relished the idea of instant, innocent infidelity. Lola could tell him more of Rose, of her dying mother. Lola, platonic Lola, Rose's friend . . . All parties would understand.

'I just might,' said Lola with maddening cool. 'I'll see how I feel.'

She arrived two hours later, took her customary position on the floor as if she had never been away. The room was full again. Gerald poured glasses of wine. Almost at once Lola broke the news.

'Rose loves you,' she said. 'Exceedingly.'

Gerald raised an eyebrow. He reflected with some wonder on the swiftness of communication between women friends. Lola was smiling, sympathetic.

'Oh yes,' she was saying. 'Rose hasn't been so bowled over

for years. Ever, perhaps. I had a feeling, didn't I, you two would get on together?'

'I remember.' Gerald sat down, rather enjoying himself. He wouldn't have minded hearing more. He searched for some way to convey his own modest feelings about the whole matter.

'Isn't she being a little . . . precipitate?' he asked. Perhaps he should have said rash, daft, or infatuated.

'Good heavens, no. How unromantic you are. I mean, you just know some things immediately, don't you?'

Gerald, who was always unsure of his initial reactions, had not the heart to disagree. 'Perhaps,' he said, feebly. 'But she indicated nothing of this to me, though she was very kind.' He glanced round the room at the neat piles of books, the vases of flowers. 'She kept you in touch with activities, did she?'

'Oh, we tell each other everything. Always have. That's why I didn't ring, knowing she was here.'

It might have been Gerald's imagination, due to the lateness of the hour, but he detected the slightest falter in this explanation of her silence. Lola now lowered her eyes.

'She told me you were potentially marvellous in bed, if a bit out of practice, and wonderfully considerate in most other ways.'

'Did she indeed?' Pride mixed with fury rose within Gerald. Was there no such thing as a discreet woman? A woman who had some respect for private moments?

Struggling for control, he murmured, 'I'm forced to believe that events can only be confirmed in a woman's mind by reporting them. A man has faith in his own private reflections, memories. They can be real to him alone. That seems to me the essential difference between the sexes.'

'Are you cross?' Lola looked at him. Such innocence.

'Cross? Not cross at all. Flattered, perhaps, I should have been the subject of your talk.'

He bent forward, stretched a hand to the back of Lola's neck. Had she not been Rose's friend he would have ravished her on the spot. As it was, her quiet presence filled him with a nameless longing that the past days and nights with Rose had done nothing to dispel.

'Rose,' said Lola, apparently unaware of his hand, 'is the most remarkable girl I know.'

'That's just what she said about you.'

'Oh, we're very loyal.' Lola gently removed his hand. 'Poor Rose. Her mother's been a burden one way and another all her life.'

'Will she be long dying?'

'She might be.' Lola lowered her eyelids again.

'In that case . . .'

'For heaven's sake, don't make some crappy suggestion about consoling each other while she's away.'

'Of course not.' The sharpness of Lola's tone suggested to Gerald it was time he became master. Against all instinct he stood up. 'I think you'd better go,' he said. 'I've a hard day tomorrow.'

'I'm sorry,' said Lola. For a split second she screwed up her eyes, disguising an almost discernible look of pain. She rose to her feet. 'I won't keep you. You must be exhausted.'

Gerald followed her to the front door, head bowed. His attempted brusqueness, meant to conceal his own temptation, had misfired. He had hurt, inadvertently, where he had meant merely to warn: to indicate he was a man of high principle where friends were concerned.

'I'll ring you,' he said gloomily.

'Oh, if you feel like it.'

Lola ran down the path into yet more spinning snow. Back in his room, Gerald had two more drinks to induce sleep, and to clear his mind. Eventually, dawn paling the snowy windows, he fell asleep, a confused man. The images of two girls raced behind his eyes – sharply, at first, figures from memory. Gradually, they dissolved into the stuff of dreams: interchanged, beckoned, laughed, teased, and faded when he touched them.

Days went by. A card came from Yorkshire.

This business may take some weeks, wrote Rose. *Please don't quite forget me.*

Gerald wondered if her echoing of Katharine Mansfield's dying words had been intentional.

30

I won't, he wrote back. *Memory of your presence lives uncomfortably in my flat.*

He was unsure whether that was the whole truth, the explanation for his restlessness. But he posted the card and rang Lola. Her silence was frustrating. Her evident pleasure, on hearing him, was cheering.

He drove her to Hungerford, on Sunday, for lunch at The Bear. She, like Rose, had a fur coat: older, softer. She refused to take it off till halfway through lunch.

'But I thought you never felt the cold,' said Gerald.

'I did today.' She sounded sad, struggled reluctantly out of its arms. Beneath it she wore an apricot silk shirt. Gathers from a deep yoke swelled over her breasts. Gerald swore he could see one of them moving, thumped by her heart. He wanted to touch it. Instead he dug into his treacle tart, eyes down, not daring to look further.

'Rose misses you *dreadfully*,' Lola was saying. 'She rings me up most evenings to ask how you are. I keep telling her I don't know, I don't see you. She keeps saying, *Do* see him, and let me have some news. That's why I came today, so that I can report back.'

'Oh.'

Gerald allowed himself the merest glance at Lola's hazel eyes, the long thick lashes cast down to indicate her seriousness.

'I suppose I shouldn't be telling you all this.'

'Probably not.'

'Do you love her?'

'Love her?' Gerald was thinking about the middle-aged couple at the next table. What had induced the woman, dressing that morning, to choose a pink velour hat, manacled by brown feathers, for a December lunch in Hungerford? 'Love her?' he repeated. 'Well, I like to think the onset of real love, when it comes, is quite clear. For the moment, I'm confused by Rose, so that can't mean love.'

'But I suppose that means some *hope*,' said Lola. 'I suppose that means some reason for optimism on Rose's part.' She smiled enchantingly. 'I mean, confusion could always *broaden out* into absolute clarity, couldn't it?'

'I suppose it could,' said Gerald, not wanting to disappoint

31

her. Then he suggested large brandies against the cold of the afternoon.

They walked on the Downs making tracks through the snow. Each kept their hands deep in their pockets. The sky, thick with more approaching snow, was broken on the horizon by zests of yellow cloud. Gerald, surprising himself, flung his greatcoat on to the ground. It made a strange patch of colour on all the white.

'God couldn't find any matching material,' giggled Lola, voicing succinctly the vaguely similar thoughts he had been having himself. He watched as Lola lowered herself on to the coat, gathering her long legs under her arms. She was protected by a hedge of snow a few inches high. She looked up at him, concerned. 'Aren't you cold?'

The wintry chill seeped through Gerald's tweed coat, a strange pleasure.

'Not at all.' He sat down beside her.

'As a matter of fact, there's nothing more elusive than clarity,' she was saying.

Again, Gerald's own thoughts: though he felt it would be feeble to agree out loud. He moved his eyes from the valley beneath them, the black-boned trees softened by the distance, to Lola's flushed face. He felt his way beneath her fur coat, beneath the warm silk of her shirt. The sky crushed down low over their heads. Gerald was surprised to find his hand suddenly on a bare thigh, pinned there by flakes of snow. He felt them melting, the water trickling between his fingers. Lola gave a shriek as it reached her flesh. There was a small thread of sound from a distant train. The bellow from an invisible cow, startling.

'This isn't right,' said Lola. But she lay back, eyes shut, snow covering her so quickly Gerald was forced to move himself on top of her to protect her from the thickening flakes.

They returned to The Bear for tea. Lola was ravenously hungry. The lady with the feathered hat sat drowsily by the fire, cup of tea in pink hand, exhausted by the indolence of her afternoon. Her companion, a small grey-flannel man, pecked at a pipe, staring at some private distance. At the sight of Gerald and Lola he looked for a moment quite shocked, as if something about them caused painful nostalgia. He tapped his pipe so savagely on the hearth that the fat lady murmured, 'Whatever is it, dear?'

When he made no reply she patted her hat for comfort so that the feathers stirred broodily and the bald patches of pink velour showed beneath.

'You must think very carefully about Rose,' said Lola, spreading honey thickly on to warm toast.

'I will, but not now.'

'You must realise she's very good at loving. She could make you extremely happy, believe me.'

Gerald put his hand on Lola's knee. She removed it at once. Exactly an hour ago she had encouraged it so hard Gerald had felt clear madness. Now there was confusing sanity. He sighed.

'What's the matter?' Lola was quite impatient, interested only in her food.

'Don't let's talk about Rose any more today. I'll think about her when you've gone.'

'Good. You'll have a bit of time. I've got to be in Paris for a week.' A perverse thrill shot through Gerald.

'Then I might even go and see her.'

'That would be best of all. You might realise.' Lola swallowed a long draught of tea, sounded practical. 'But please don't do it in the snow.'

"Course not. Idiot. What do you think I am?'

'An unintentional menace,' she said, 'trying to please us all.'

Gerald was not quite able to keep his word. In Yorkshire the following weekend, her dying mother in a bedroom upstairs, Rose reacted with such exuberant pleasure he wondered how he had survived the last couple of weeks without her. She managed to disguise the strains caused upon the household by illness. He admired her for that. All she asked, in deference to her mother, was that he should keep to his own room at night. To this Gerald unwillingly concurred, increasingly desirous of the warm, slightly plumper Rose, so strong in her concealment of melancholy.

On the Saturday afternoon they went for a walk on the moors near Haworth. The earth was scarred with the last

33

remnants of snow: there was rain in the wind. They clung to each other, faces stinging in the cold. Scarcely speaking, they tramped for several miles, then took shelter from a heavy shower under trees. Gerald laid his coat on the hard dry earth: the familiarity of the gesture reminded him of his promise, and of the recent coupling on the wintry Downs. He hesitated only for a moment. Rose was kissing his hair, scrabbling at his shirt, muttering words of love. Succumbing to her, he heard only the rain on the leaves: no thought of Lola.

Later, wiping rain from Rose's cheeks with his handkerchief, came a moment of revelation. Rose was the girl for him: nothing had ever been so clear in his life. Desire quite sated, he felt love for her, though he said nothing for fear of her over-brimming with pleasure. She had mud on her mackintosh and tears in her eyes: had never looked more vulnerable and trusting. He wondered if he should make an instant proposal of marriage, while the inspiration was upon him. Then Rose sneezed, smothered her face in a damp handkerchief, and the moment had gone.

'I expect you and Lola . . .' she said, and paused. 'Have you?'

Gerald said nothing, made an attempt to twist his cold face into an expression of surprise.

Rose took his hand. 'Not that I mind,' she went on, mouth turned down. 'Don't ever think that. Lola's my friend. All I'd ever ask is the truth, that's all. I can't bear the idea of deception.'

'Quite,' said Gerald, and the clarity he had felt only minutes before disappeared.

He watched a black cloud roll across a nearby ridge of land, obscuring it, and was suddenly depressed by the sound of rain. It occurred to him that the post he had been offered in Rio might be the solution. If he went abroad for a couple of years he would forget them, they would forget him. He'd come back to find them both married, be willing godfather to their children.

'Lola likes you very much indeed,' Rose was saying. 'You must know that, don't you? Really, she'd be much better for you than me. She'd keep you guessing for years, never wholly committing herself. That's what men like, isn't it? Seems to me

34

the last thing in the world they want is the whole of someone: only selected parts. That's where Lola's so skilful. She'd never burden you with the whole of herself. Afraid I could never be like that. Loving someone, I can't resist offering them the entire package, keeping nothing back. I suppose that's awfully boring but I can't help it.' She laughed a little. 'So, really, there should be no confusion in your mind.'

Gerald remained silent for a few moments, struggling to do up the knot of his tie. Then he said, 'It's a little overwhelming, after two years with no one in my life, suddenly to find two new friends who seem so kind and caring.'

'Two new friends,' repeated Rose. 'But you met Lola first. You liked Lola first.'

'I made love to you first.' He tried to be honest. 'I feel closer to you.'

'Really?' Rose pressed herself against him, soft with relief. He wished she would get up, change the conversation.

'Don't see why there should be any complications,' he said, finally. 'Shouldn't we be getting back? We're both frozen.'

Rose had the good sense to agree at once. They spoke no more of Lola, spent a peaceful Sunday by the fire, both aware of a new bond of understanding.

Gerald returned to London with reluctance. He missed Rose as soon as the train drew out of the station. But, back in the silence of his flat, his thoughts turned to Lola. It was her he wanted, most urgently, beside him in the room. He rang her flat but there was no reply. So instead he rang Rose. Her surprise and pleasure cheered him, though the confusion remained. Wearily, he went early to bed and dreamed of the freedom of Rio.

Rose returned to London as soon as she could after her mother's death. She arranged an immediate meeting with Lola. They sat in opposite corners of a battered sofa that had come from Lola's nursery, and for years had been their favourite place for serious talk. Each noted the other's pale face. They equipped themselves with large drinks, which was not their normal custom.

'I only got back from Paris last night,' said Lola, 'so I haven't heard from Gerald how it all was.'

'Harrassing. She seemed to go mad, the last week. Insulted me hour after hour but wouldn't let me leave her bedside. Gerald came up for a few days. He was . . .' She paused, wanting to say loving. 'Noble,' she said.

'I can imagine. It must have been difficult for you, the house so gloomy and quiet.'

Rose was near to smiling. 'We slipped off,' she said, 'for the occasional reviving walk. Over the moors.'

A long silence. Their eyes did not meet.

'Was it snowing, up there?' Lola asked eventually.

'Snowing? Well, there was snow on the ground. No, but it rained a lot. Why?'

Lola thought for a while. She decided, for the first time, that the whole truth would not benefit her friend. 'He said he particularly liked going for bitter walks in the snow.'

'He's a funny one, all right,' said Rose. 'What are we going to do about him, Lo?'

Now Rose had come to the point, Lola stretched her long legs with relief. The gin was beginning to turn her blood warmly to quicksilver. It would be quite easy, now, as such old friends, to be practical. They could solve the problem very quickly.

'It's quite clear we both love him,' she said, 'and it's quite clear he loves both of us. All we've got to do is force his hand in making a choice. Procrastination is the destructive thing. Hell, the greatest friends on earth could hardly be expected to survive the misery he's causing us, waiting for his decision.'

'To be fair, he's only known us a couple of months, hasn't he? Perhaps,' she smiled, incredulous, 'I mean, it could be he doesn't want *either* of us.'

'Nonsense,' scoffed Lola. Rose copied the brusque, practical tone of her friend's voice.

'Well, *my* position is quite clear,' she said. 'I want to marry him.'

'Do you? *Marry* him? Marry him? – I suppose that's what I'd like too,' said Lola.

'He's the only man on earth *I* could possibly contemplate marrying.'

36

'Well, you're ahead,' said Lola. 'He feels closer to you, easier with you.'

'But you frighten him more, and that intrigues him. You're the mystery figure. I'm the warm open book.'

They both laughed.

'Put a shotgun at his head and there's little doubt who he'd choose,' said Lola. 'Oh God, why on earth did this have to happen? And, more interesting, what is it that we love him for? Sometimes, I just can't think.'

'Nor I,' said Rose. 'After all, he's balding, unfit, drinks too much, pompous, vague, and possibly deceitful.'

'Too short,' added Lola. 'Awful breath after Sunday lunch, hideous shoes, drives dangerously, boasts boringly about his lack of friends. There's absolutely nothing I can think of, on the face of it, to recommend him.'

'Except that his sympathy is overwhelming, and he makes me laugh.'

'And also,' said Lola, screwing up her face with the effort of choosing the right words, 'he has this extraordinary, understated relish in perfectly ordinary things. In his presence you feel the urgency of every day, somehow: the pointlessness of wasting time. Do you know what I mean? We've never discussed any of this, of course. He'd be loath to do any such thing, I'm sure, and so would I.'

Rose nodded. 'In a subtle way,' she added, 'not by paying obvious compliments, he boosts the morale. Makes you feel *better* than you imagined you could about yourself.'

'All of which,' said Lola, 'cancels out the mild deficiencies.' They both smiled, and were silent for a while.

The telephone rang. Lola leaned back on the sofa, eyes shut, not moving. When eventually it stopped, she turned her head almost sleepily to Rose.

'You deserve him,' she said. 'I can just back out quietly. Not see him any more till you're married, or whatever.'

'Nonsense,' said Rose. 'He'd be far happier with you. Endlessly intrigued. Honestly.'

'Rubbish,' said Lola. 'I'd drive him mad.'

'He'd be bored to tears by my constant enthusiasm. Smothered by my open love. He'd be – '

Getting up, Lola cut her short. 'This is utterly ridiculous,

Rosie,' she said. 'Why not let's resolve it immediately?' She
looked at her watch. 'He must be at home. Let's go round
now. Make him come to some conclusion.'

'Isn't that a bit unfair, giving him no warning?' Rose, for all
her reluctance, stood up too.

'It's less unfair than carrying on like this. It may all end in
disaster, but at least you and I can go back to where we were.
That's what I really mind about.'

'Me too,' said Rose.

Giving themselves no time to change their minds, they left
the flat very quickly.

Gerald spent a most disagreeable evening. The gas fire produced no heat in his bitter room, there was nothing but stale
cheese in the fridge. He was depressed by the unmade bed,
the dust, the mess, the general lack of care that had increased
since Rose's departure. He rang her, feeling a decent amount
of days had passed since her mother's funeral: a little house-
work would take her mind off things, and he would reward
her with a delicious dinner in some expensive restaurant.
When there was no reply from her flat a vague uneasiness
disturbed him. Where was this girl? Just when he needed her
most. He rang several times, became increasingly irritated by
the lack of reply. Finally, angry, he ate cold baked beans with
the cheese, and rang Lola. Her presence, suddenly, seemed
even more desirable than Rose's. She wouldn't offer to clear
up, but her funny smile, in her place by the fire, would restore
tranquillity. Besides, it was high time they renewed their carnal
acquaintance in a place more comfortable than a snowy Down.
Lola must be there, and come quickly. Goddammit, he loved
the girl. The fact was astoundingly clear. He must do something about it quickly, before he booked himself a passage to
Rio.

But there was no reply from Lola, either. He was let down
on all sides, deserted, forlorn. Implacable. With no heart to
study his briefs for the court case next day, or to read a book
or listen to music, Gerald poured himself a large whisky and
burrowed into his chair by the hissing fire. In the bleak hours
that followed, moon glaring through the windows, some semi-
wakeful dream of a composite girl teased his mind. Wearily,

38

he followed her movements: watched the heaving of Lola's bosom, the twinkle in Rose's eye – found a hand in his he could not identify, smaller than Lola's but larger than Rose's. There was a singular flash of pure Lola as she was the first night he had seen her, tall and aloof, scorning the winter air that made the others shiver. This was followed by a view of Rose, too, alone, radiating in the sombre hall of her mother's house. Then the two figures merged again, confusing, taunting.

'To hell with you both,' he shouted out loud, stirring himself, the words flat and blurred in the silence.

He reached for yet another drink but found the bottle empty. His hands were stiff and cold: he rubbed them hopelessly together, trying to summon the energy to go to the cupboard for a new bottle of whisky. Then, from the profundities of his desolate state, he heard the far-off ring of his front door bell. He let it ring several times, to make sure it was not a further trick of the imagination, then struggled to his feet. He experienced a moment of being grateful to his education and upbringing: when called upon, however low, a man can and must make an effort. He straightened his tie, adjusted the look of discontent he could feel dragging at his face, and with supreme effort cast self-pity aside. Whoever was calling at his door would see a calm and satisfied man, a man whose own resources were enough. Pleased with this sudden transformation of his person, the gallant Gerald made for the stairs, new confidence ensuring a firm and eager step.

Lola and Rose stood there, inevitable snow on their hair and shoulders. Something united about them, something determined. Gerald forced a smile.

'Come in,' he said. 'Come in, come in, come in.'

They followed him up the stairs in silence, kept on their coats, took their places on the floor in front of the fire. Gerald poured three drinks, took his place in his own chair. Through the confusion in his head, he sensed their silence was a little ominous. Perhaps they had some important matter about which they wished him to adjudicate: he was their friendly lawyer, after all. But if this was the case, Gerald felt perversely unhelpful. He would do nothing to broach the subject of their difficulty. From a befuddled distance he would watch them struggle, sipping his drink all the while. Might even enjoy himself. But they said nothing. Eventually, his natural instinct to assist overcoming less charitable feelings, Gerald muttered, 'Well?'

Lola drew herself up then, her long neck a gleaming white stem in the dim light. Her nostrils flared as they did sometimes, Gerald had noticed, when she was worried. A line of boyhood poetry came back to him. *The camels sniff the evening air* . . . Shelley, was it?

'We've got to get this all sorted out, Gerald,' she said.

Gerald heard his own sigh of relief. All his life people had required him to sort things out. In his childhood, the drone of bombers over High Wycombe, there had been the matter of his socks. These, in the opinion of his old nanny, needed sorting out most days of the week. Gerald obliged, of course, without demur, rather enjoying marshalling the balls of red, blue and grey wool into strict soldier lines in his drawer. And Nanny had always praised him. In his teens he had something of a reputation for sorting out fights between dogs – due to a combination of his quick draw on a soda syphon, and his authoritative voice. After his father died, having sorted out the muddled will, he turned to sorting out his mother's lovers, placating the rejects and warning the present incumbent his position was likely to be temporary. Little wonder, then, he eventually turned his skills to professional use. Only a decent humility kept him from reflecting upon the number of his grateful clients, whose complex problems he had successfully sorted out over the years.

Whatever Lola had in mind, then, would be a routine matter.

'How can I help?' he asked, recognising the sympathetic tone he used in the office when meeting with a new client.

'You can decide.' Lola's response was quick, fierce.

'You can clear up the confusion once and for all,' followed Rose, 'and put an end to this misery.' She, too, was unnaturally fierce.

'Confusion?' asked Gerald, mystified.

'Don't try to be silly, Gerald,' said Lola. 'Don't try to pretend you don't know what we're on about.'

Gerald tipped back his head into the familiar, comforting dip of a velvet cushion. He shut his eyes. The old thought came to

40

him that there is a deviousness about the demands of women that confuses the straightest man. To deal seriously with them, superhuman patience and tact must be called upon. It was very late at night to summon such energies, but Rose and Lola were his friends. He would try. He would cast aside all the burning logic of his own mind and attempt not only to understand but also to feel the torments of theirs. That way, as he had come to learn in his practice, is the best short cut to sorting out.

He opened his eyes. 'If you could tell me more,' he said, 'perhaps I could – '

'We both love you, idiot,' Rose interrupted. 'And it's plain you love both of us. Which one of us do you want?'

Gerald looked from her face to Lola's. In both their beautiful eyes he saw the same, naked love glowering through a thin film of hostility. He shivered, repeated the question silently to himself. Funny how he had not confronted himself with the actual question before. Now, faced with it, his responsive mind, for all the whisky, was concentrated wonderfully. Which one did he want? If indeed he wanted either. And if he did, what would he want her *for*? Life? Marriage? A divorce wrangle in court in ten years' time? God forbid: it would be better to remain friends with both. Platonic, if need be. If that was what was depressing them, the sharing of carnality. Women friends, as he well knew, had their limitations when it came to sharing a man.

'There doesn't seem to me much problem does there?' he said, his voice unconvincing. 'Surely there's no need for any such severing choice? Surely we can carry on as we are, all good – '

His final feeble word was lost in their hoots of derision, their scornful laughs.

'How can you *demean* yourself with such a suggestion?' shouted Lola.

'Does it never occur to you,' shrieked Rose, 'what you are doing? Lola and I have been friends for *years*, you know. For God's sake, you've made gestures to us both. You've turned to us both, relied on us both, indicated you love us both . . . *Which one do you want?*'

They gave him a moment's silence in which to reflect and

41

reply. But when he made no response they started up again, interrupting each other, repeating themselves. The questions came so fast there was no hope of Gerald contributing a thought, had he had anything to say – which, for once in his life, when it came to sorting out a problem, he hadn't. He was aware of a great desire to laugh. The situation, from his point of view, was highly comic: two beautiful women screaming at him to choose one of them, fired by their presumption that he loved both of them. Well, he did in a way. But love for anyone is an irregular graph, and while he would not deny that at moments his feelings for both of them had whizzed up the chart into astonishing peaks, for the moment they had caught him at a real low – tired, hungry, depressed, a little drunk. The warm adrenalin of certainty, which he presumed should accompany any major decision a man takes concerning the binding of his life to one woman, was far from him. All he desired was that they should leave him in peace, now. He would think about the matter for the rest of the night, and write to them both in the morning. He could book a ticket . . . They were glaring at him, silent at last.

Gerald heard himself give a small, friendly laugh, and felt his dry lips crackle into a small matching smile.

'Well,' he said at last. 'Why don't you toss for me?' His suggestion charged the silence with explosive fury.

'We're in no mood for jokes, Gerald,' said Lola.

'No, we're not,' said Rose.

Gerald wished they could see their own faces, wizened and glowing with anger. God, they were beautiful, each one in her own way. He felt terrible desire for them both. Then, in the moment of fighting that desire, an inspiration came to him. There was no time to prepare its presentation. He would put it very simply, eyes shut to make it easier.

'You could run a race for me,' he said.

When eventually he opened his eyes, two new expressions confronted him: indignation, yes; but indignation softened at the edges, as if *possibility* danced lightly in the background.

'Run a *race* for you?' Lola's huge mothy eyes enlarged in a very good show of incredulity.

'A race for you?' echoed Rose. And then she surprised. 'But we're so unfit,' she said, quietly.

42

'We haven't run for years,' agreed Lola.

Taking these observations for some kind of concession, Gerald saw his way ahead was no easier.

'There could be *time*,' he suggested generously. 'Heavens, there's no hurry, is there? You could train. A month, say. Two if you like. Meanwhile, I'll work out a nice little cross-country course. Nothing too strenuous. About five miles . . .'

'*Gerald*.' Lola's voice was weak, her head bent so appealingly on one shoulder Gerald was much tempted to lean over and restore it to its rightful upright position, kissing her all the while.

'Gerald, really,' said Rose, who was always less sparing with words, and a single tear slid down her cheek.

Filled with new strength, heartened by the attraction of his own idea, Gerald felt he should make some effort to console, comfort, convince.

'It may seem an absurd plan on the face of it,' he began, with all the sparkle of one who doesn't believe a word he's saying, 'but if you think of it – it's probably the only solution. I mean, the only fair solution. You see – and forgive me if this sounds lacking in courage, but I'm inexperienced when it comes to deciding about women – I wouldn't like to hold myself responsible. I wouldn't, I couldn't, choose. You must see that, don't you? You must understand what a dilemma you've caused me.' He took a deep, determined breath. 'You must see what . . . affection I have for you both. How pleased I'd be to be married to either of you.' Both girls gave small snorts of protest, but the fight seemed to have gone out of them. 'In the circumstances, for my own part, I'd be quite pleased to carry on as we have been: all three of us friends. But I do see your point, of course I do. I understand the difficulties. So it seems to me my solution isn't a bad one. It might even be rather fun.' He looked from one to the other of them. 'But then again you might have all sorts of objections. In that case . . . I suppose the only thing to do would be to say goodbye to you both. I'm very tempted by a job in Rio. With you both gone, there'd be nothing much to keep me here.'

It was by now nearly five in the morning, the sky through the bare windows a grimy colour, the girls' faces drawn and shadowy. Lola, in her usual position on her knees by the fire,

43

let a small silence pass when Gerald had finished speaking, then swivelled a defiant head towards Rose.

'What d'you think, Rosie? I'm game.'

Rose gasped. '*Lo*. You can't . . . I mean, you realise what it'd involve, the result? Whoever won – whoever got Gerald – it would be the end of us.'

'I know,' said Lola.

Rose's acceptance was barely audible. 'Very well,' she said. 'But it's the most terrible plan I've ever heard.'

'It is,' said Lola, with such bitterness that Gerald's heart briefly contracted with fear, 'but on the other hand, Gerald is right. Too feeble to make the decision himself, we have to make it for him. We might as well give him a little amusement on the way.'

'I suppose so.' Rose was equally hard. She looked at Gerald. 'But anything rather than Rio.'

'Yes, well, that's decided then.'

Gerald feared more discussion might undo the decision. But his fears were allayed by Lola's tone of practicality as, standing, she said, 'A month, then. Rosie was always faster than me cross-country. A minute's start would be fair for me, wouldn't it, Rosie?'

'Quite fair.'

'It'll all be *scrupulously* fair,' assured Gerald. 'I'll plan the course with incredible care. We'll walk round it together the day before.'

'*Wonderful*,' said Lola.

'Very considerate,' said Rose.

'Oh, you can rely on me,' said Gerald.

They left him then, with no kiss on the cheek, none of the old cheerful promises to meet soon. At his gate, they paused for a moment, both cold in the unfriendly drive, though Lola let her fur coat fall open when she saw Rose pulling hers tightly round her.

'It would probably be better, Rosie, wouldn't it, not to be in touch till the day?'

'Probably it would.' Their eyes met.

'Sorry. I'm sorry.'

'For God's sake, Lo, all these years! It's ridiculous.' Rose, near to tears, shaking with cold, was shouting. 'It's the

44

maddest plan I ever heard. Why don't we just turn our backs, both of us . . . Leave him?'

'We can't do that.'

'But he doesn't deserve you, me, anyone.'

'No.'

Rose looked up at her tall, determined friend. She thought how precarious is friendship: how hopelessly threatened by things unworthy to destroy.

'Till the race, then,' she said, and turned away.

From his window Gerald watched the girls part. He felt quite awake now, the clarity of his insane plan firing him with energy and glee. Only for a moment did the idea of abandoning the whole project, writing it off as a poor late-night joke, cross his mind. A man must go ahead in his decisions. There was much to be done. Funny, though, to think that his last few weeks of bachelorhood would be spent in poring over ordnance survey maps. And come to think of it, where were those damn maps?

Gerald went to his desk, began rummaging through drawers. Enthused by the whole project of planning an interesting route – a route which would tax, but not weary to excess – Gerald was able to spare no thought, that busy dawn, for his competitors. If they were returning, troubled, to their beds, he could not conceive of their unease. He himself had no experience of the severing of friendship: mere visitor to many, he had always been a friendless man.

For Lola, training meant increasing her morning runs from three to seven days a week. Besides this, she gave up all alcohol and went to gym classes in the evening. Within a week, she felt the difference in herself: strong, alert, fit. There was no breathlessness in her runs round Hyde Park, now. In the bitter frosty mornings, unripe sun the single spot of colour in the grey air, she relished her calm, her vigour, the final reserve of energy that allowed her to sprint with astonishing speed over the last lap, from Knightsbridge Barracks to Hyde Park Corner. She had no doubt that she would win the race. As teenagers, it was true, Rose had both exceptional stamina and speed. But nowadays she took little exercise. She was

45

plump and unfit. In fact, to be fair, when the time came Lola would refuse any start. They would begin as equals and the best one would win the trophy of Gerald.

Now her training was in full swing, the absurdity of its reason had curiously evaporated from Lola's mind. She thought much of Rose, but with little guilt. After all, she had met Gerald first, had introduced them. When Rose had seduced Gerald, Lola had honourably disappeared to give them a chance. It was not her fault Gerald had not made something of his opportunity. It was to promote Rose she had accepted lunch that Sunday and found herself in an unlikely position on the Downs: an event which made clear to her the extent of the feelings she had been at such pains to conceal. Rose would make Gerald happier, of course: she was much better equipped with all the conventional aids to marital contentment. But Lola doubted if Rose could love him more. God knows why, but the idea of the rest of Lola's life without him was inconceivable. Perhaps she should have indicated this some time ago, and she would have won him without having to go through all the madness of this race. But Lola was cautious of proclamations. The uncertainty that silence causes lovers is often a more lasting bond than declared certainty. On the other hand, it, too, can be misinterpreted. Lola hoped Gerald had not misunderstood her – well, if he had, there would be a lifetime in which to make amends. For the moment she missed him intolerably. They spoke occasionally on the telephone, about matters pertaining to the race: no suggestion was ever made that the whole thing should be cancelled. And so the bleak wintry days went by, the increasing strength of her limbs Lola's only consolation. In her weaker moments she thought of Rose with regret. She missed her. One day, perhaps, there could be forgiveness all round, and they could be friends again. Meantime, the object was to beat her.

Jobless for the present, Rose decided to leave London. If the race was to be cross-country, she decided there could be no better place to train than her native moors. So she returned to Yorkshire, to the cold cheerless house that awaited a new owner, and set about her task with a sad determination. The old housekeeper was still in residence. She welcomed Rose with all the warmth of someone starved of human company. The old-fashioned kitchen flared into life again as Mrs Nichols steamed and baked to satisfy Rose's customary hunger. But Rose had no appetite. She was aware that to lose many pounds of flesh was the first necessity if she was to have any hope of winning Gerald. Besides, an icy desolation acted on her stomach like poison, so that food sickened and the long nights were sleepless. She rose early every morning, shivered into the bitter drizzly air in a thin tracksuit, and began her long jog over the dewy moors. She increased her time and distance every day, and within a week was able to rejoice in the result: all her old speed and stamina were returning. Sprinting up a steep slope, she could arrive at the top without panting for breath. On rocky, stony ground she found herself to be surprisingly sure-footed. And her speed on the flat, at the end of a long run, increased both her confidence and pride.

Her hours on the moors were free from pain except when she passed close to the place where she and Gerald had sheltered from the rain. Then, longing for him returned acutely, but could be subdued by the physical act of running. It was the hours between that caused the real torment: the dreary afternoons in the deserted house, the silence, the missing of Gerald and Lola. Rose forced herself to do exercises recommended in a Keep Fit manual, and went almost hourly to her dim mirror in search of some change in her appearance. Here she was soon rewarded. Hollow cheeks and a flat stomach indicated new fitness. The scales showed she had lost nearly a stone in two weeks. Her speed over the moors secretly surprised and amazed. Pessimism changed to optimism. One morning she woke with no doubts left: she was going to win after all. Lola was an ungainly runner with a huge stride. She had no chance against Rose in her prime, and Rose was making sure the physique of her prime was returning. She confided in Mrs Nichols, who encouraged her in the long kitchen evenings.

'You'll win, Miss Rose. There's no one with determination the like of yours. You've always won.'

Gerald rang her sometimes. She took her chance to express her unaltered love for him, in the belief that the most sensitive man is incapable of guessing accurately the measure of love he is receiving. His response was not encouraging, in that he seemed more eager to discuss matters pertaining to the race. But Rose understood: having initiated such an event, it must preoccupy his mind. Once it was over there would be a lifetime in which to regale him with declarations. She tried hard not to think of Lola, and the sadness of the future without her. But given the simple choice, who would give up a lover for a friend? Still, Rose missed Lola. Really, the whole thing was very regrettable. But of course she could not be the one to suggest they went back on the decision. One day, perhaps, there could be forgiveness all round, and they could be friends again. Meantime, the object was to beat her.

In a pub near Hungerford, Gerald was unable quite to refrain from revealing his plans, and he became something of a local hero. He found himself describing the contestants of the race and bets began to be placed. Several people who lived locally suggested to him routes – routes which would include the kind of tests that meant real excitement: high slopes, knotty wood-lands, stony ground, heavy plough . . . But the last stretch of the race was Gerald's own inspiration. The girls would end at Coombe Gibbet, the old gallows. Dwarfed by its outstretched arms, they would for a moment be etched against the winter sky. All that would be left then would be the gentle downward slope to the winning post. (Gerald had already bought a red-and-white chequered flag.) Yes, it would be a dramatic end. There would be champagne, of course, and a marvellous lunch for all three of them. After that . . . Gerald's imagination clouded. The joke over, what would happen? He would have to rely on the sportsmanship of the loser: hope she would go quietly on her way, no fuss, no tears. God knows what he would do with the winner: see her a good deal, he presumed. Get used to her. Hope that eventually she and the loser would resume their friendship. Because, in truth, the idea of losing completely either Rose *or* Lola was too terrible to contemplate. Not that Gerald spent very much time contemplating at the moment. He was wholly occupied by the planning of the route. Evenings in London were spent in the meticulous study of ordnance survey maps. Every weekend he walked the proposed route, rejecting various stretches and replacing them with others. Finally, he was satisfied. The five-mile run was full of interest, slight hazards calculated to intimidate but not to hurt. Gerald's acquaintances in the pub chuckled and agreed. They would be out in force to cheer the girls on. It would be a novel sport for a Saturday.

His plans finalised, Gerald rang Rose and Lola to break the news. He detected a certain coolness in both their voices, but put this down to nerves. Neither would consider it dignified, of course, to show enthusiasm for such an unusual venture. And both insisted on walking alone round the route with Gerald. This, he felt, was a little unreasonable: to make a man walk ten miles when he need only walk five – and heaven knows in his careful research he must have walked fifty miles by now – showed some meanness of spirit. However, bracing himself, Gerald complied with good grace. Dates were arranged.

Lola came first. Huddled in her fur coat, wool cap pulled low over her face, it was hard to tell the state of her fitness. Gerald welcomed her with all his old warmth.

Lola did not respond. 'Let's get on with it,' was all she said. Obligingly Gerald opened a gate.

'Won't be opening it on the day,' he grinned. 'You can get over it any way you like – jump, vault, climb – '

'Quite,' snapped Lola.

From time to time Gerald attempted to make a joke, to assume light-heartedness. But meeting with total silence he eventually gave up, and was reduced merely to explaining the way. Back at the winning post at last, the afternoon sky low with threatened rain, he gave Lola a map with the route thoughtfully marked in red pencil. So she could learn it off by heart, he explained. But now, how about some tea at The Bear?

Lola declined at once, and moved towards her car which was parked in a nearby lane. Gerald opened the door for her, brushed her cold hard cheek with his lips. She softened for the merest second.

'Oh God,' she said. 'You know this is insanity, Gerald, don't you?'

'Don't worry,' said Gerald. 'Thing is, don't take it too seriously. It'll be a lot of fun.'

When Lola had driven away, three prospective betting men, gumbooted and heavily clad in mackintoshes, appeared in much good humour from behind a hedge. They had been studying the form, they explained: nice little runner, this one. Lovely flanks, strong legs. Much laughter over subsequent drinks. They, at any rate, had entered into the spirit of the thing. It was only later, as he drove back to London, that Gerald recalled Lola's parting face, and wondered if, secretly, she was afraid.

Rose came two days later. Fur-coated too, but hollow-cheeked.

'Taken your training seriously, have you?' Gerald enquired.

But Rose responded with no more warmth than Lola. On their walk round the course – and Rose bounded along at an impressive pace so that Gerald found himself quite puffed, trying to keep up with her – she only broke her silence once, to enquire about the crossing of a stream.

'Are we meant to jump it or run through it?'

Gerald had given no thought as to which he required, but felt it best to be instantly decisive.

'Jump,' he said, noting the slippery banks. That would make for a little more fun. Rose screwed up her enormous eyes: Gerald had forgotten their intense green.

'Jump?' she repeated, in a small voice.

'Or you could . . .' he wavered.

'No, no. It's all right. Jump, you say.' She seemed a million miles away.

Back at the winning post Rose, too, was offered tea and declined. She wished instead to be driven straight back to the station.

In the car she said, 'I'm terrified I'll never remember the way.'

'You study that map,' advised Gerald, 'and you'll know it by heart. Besides, there'll be signs. White flags, pointing. Also, a few people, I dare say, to cheer you on –'

'People?'

'Well. You know how it is. Things get around. It'll add to the excitement.'

50

'God Almighty,' said Rose, weakly. 'I thought it was going to be an entirely private matter.'

On the empty platform, she looked peculiarly small.

'Don't wait,' she said. Gerald turned to go, understanding he was genuinely not wanted. 'But do say goodbye.' He turned back to kiss her, confused. 'I'll love you for ever, anyway,' she said. 'Don't forget that.'

Hurrying off to meet his new friends in the pub, Gerald felt a distinct and alarming hunch: he knew who was going to win, and tears hurt his eyes. Of course, he could be wrong. He needed to know what the others reckoned. They had studied Rose, too, from their position behind a hawthorn hedge. Having done so, what were the odds on her? Gerald drove recklessly fast through the town to the pub, keen to know.

The morning of the race, Gerald arrived first, an hour before it was scheduled to begin. He had made sure not to ask either competitor how they were transporting themselves to this remote area of the Downs – it was none of his business – and he had no idea what to expect. He felt briefly guilty about Rose. She did not have a car. But no doubt a taxi could be found at Hungerford station.

It was a cold, bright morning. Sharp sun, pale sky; earth hard from overnight frost, bare branches still glittering where the rime had not melted. Perfect conditions. Gerald, clumsy in his old army greatcoat, banged his sides with his arms, stamped his feet and blew on his hands. He watched the globes of breath launch forth bold as Atlantic balloonists, only to disintegrate without trace seconds later. He smiled to himself, well pleased.

He collected things from the car – stopwatch, ordnance survey map with the route meticulously marked in red, flasks of coffee and brandy. These would keep him going till lunch. He had ordered Black Velvets and steak-and-kidney pudding to be waiting for himself, Rose and Lola in The Bear. God knows what sort of a lunch that would be, but there was no use in speculating. With any luck, the joke over, they would all go their own ways. Gerald had refrained from thinking about the future – uneasy subject in the circumstances – but in the back of his mind was a plan to visit his mother in Ireland. Time would be needed for reflection. On his return he would get in touch with the winner, being an honourable man, and see how things went from there.

A Land Rover arrived. It contained four men in tweed jackets and sturdy boots. They had placed considerable bets on the race. Two of them carried binoculars, the others prodded their shooting sticks into the earth, testing its state. They banged Gerald on the back, offered him brandy from their flasks, and made jokes in loud voices. They were out for a good morning's sport and Gerald, responsible for their pleasure, felt himself something of a hero. Cheered by the sudden companionship, he entered into the spirit of the thing, and presumed himself temporarily to be among friends.

Others arrived. The news, it seemed, had travelled. They stood about, thumping themselves to keep warm, asking permission to study Gerald's map spread on the bonnet of his car. Gerald heard only one dissident voice among them. A fierce lean girl in leather went from group to group haranguing them about being male chauvinist pigs: but she was powerless to spoil their fun. 'Ah, it's a bit of sport, girl,' explained one of the tweedies, gently punching the breastless leather jacket. Alone in her opinion, she eventually went away.

At five to eleven, no sign of the competitors, Gerald felt the first stirrings of anxiety. There were jokes about sudden withdrawal. New bets were placed about whether the runners would turn up at all.

But at eleven o'clock precisely, Lola's red Mini drove through the gate. Amazed, Gerald watched both her and Rose get out of the car. As far as he knew, they hadn't communicated since the night of the decision. The implications of their drive down from London together was suddenly moving. He gave himself a moment to recover before striding over to greet them. Both girls wore their fur coats, bright wool socks and expensive running shoes, very new. Both had their hair scraped back, and large, unmade-up eyes. They looked about at the gathered spectators, registered horror. Then, unsmiling, turned simultaneously to Gerald.

'We thought this was to be a private event,' said Lola.

Gerald shrugged. 'Well, I'm sorry. You know how things get about.'

'It's appalling,' said Rose.

'You'll be quite unaware of them,' explained Gerald, 'once you get going. Anyway, it's rather encouraging, isn't it, to have an audience cheering you on?'

Neither girl replied. Gerald offered them coffee, brandy, biscuits. They refused everything. They stood closely together, arms just touching, a little sullen. Noting their faces, regret, sudden and consuming, chilled Gerald more deeply than the raw air. He would have given anything to have withdrawn from the whole silly idea . . . But then Lola gave him an unexpected smile, and he detected Rose's look as almost compassionate.

'Come on, then, let's get it over,' said Lola.

Gerald's spirits returned. He should have had no worries. They, too, saw it as no more than a lark: something that would make a good story for years to come.

'I've ordered a stupendous lunch for us all at The Bear,' he said gratefully, and was puzzled they conveyed no gratitude in return.

Brusquely, they flung their coats into Lola's car. Their clothes beneath were almost identical: shorts and tee-shirts. Lola's had *I'm no hero* stamped across her large bosom. Rose's tee-shirt bore the message *Like me*. Gerald wondered if these messages were part of some private plan between them. He noted the paleness of their limbs, and the way their skin shrivelled into gooseflesh. Rose hugged herself, shivering. Lola left her arms at her side, characteristically defying the sharp air. Both looked remarkably fit. Rose was much thinner. Muscles rippled up Lola's long thighs.

Gerald took off his tie, which was to be the starting line – an amateur detail symbolising the *fun* of the whole thing, he thought. He walked a few paces up the slope, placed it on the ground. Standing again, he took in the sweep of misty country-side beneath them, shafts of sun stabbing into plough and trees.

'Now, you know where you have to go?' Both girls nodded. 'No problems about the course? Don't think you can go wrong.

There are signs all along the route. Put them up myself yesterday.'

He bent over to tweak the tie, make certain it was straight. The girls were prancing up and down, now, bending their knees and sniffing.

'Right,' said Gerald. 'I understand you've decided Lola shouldn't have a start after all.'

'Right,' said Rose. 'She'll gain up the hills.'

'There's absolutely nothing between us,' said Lola.

'Quite sure about that?' Gerald was determined to be absolutely fair.

'Very well, then. Are you ready? Good luck to you both.'

Simultaneously, Rose and Lola both crouched low over the tie, fingers just touching it. Gerald let his eyes travel up and down their spines, knobbly through the thin stuff of their tee-shirts. He remembered the feel of both their backs.

Standing at attention to one side of the tie, he saw Rose's bent knee wobble, and a drip on Lola's nose. Never had either girl looked more desirable. But nothing in his voice – his old Sandhurst shout suddenly called to aid – gave any hint of such sentiments.

'On your marks,' he bellowed, 'get set. *Go!*'

Both girls leapt up, matching flames, Gerald thought. Breasts thrust forward, heads back, nostrils wide. They ran slowly away from him, side by side through the silver grass. A cheer went up from the crowd. Laughter. Melting frost still sparkled. Gerald kept his eyes on the competitors, almost out of sight now, buttocks twisting in their identical white shorts.

When they had rounded the first bend, Gerald returned to his car. He drove to a wood half a mile away. He knew he would be able to see their approach from a long way off. Other spectators had reached the wood before him. They cheered as his car passed, waved with menacing glee. Sensing a small flicker of shame, Gerald ignored them. Did not wave back.

His parking place was deserted. Relieved, he sat on the bonnet and focused his binoculars on the distant path. Sunbeams knifed the fading mists about him, jabbing through branches and tree trunks, so that for a moment he suffered the illusion he was trapped in a cage of slanting golden bars.

The distant crackle of undergrowth: through his glasses,

54

Gerald could just see them, now, in focus. Lola a little ahead, mud-splattered legs in spite of the hard ground – strands of escaped hair across her brow. Rose's thighs were alarmingly pink, mottled with purple discs. Gerald felt himself smiling. They made a fine pair, and one of them would make a fine wife. Unbelievable, really, to think *they were racing to win him*. He was to be the trophy, the husband! Did he care which one became his? At this moment he did not. They both looked equally touching, running so eagerly. Either would do.

As they approached, neither Rose nor Lola glanced his way. Good girls: that was the way to win races. Concentration. And conservation of energy. For the moment, both seemed to have plenty of that in reserve. They were admirably calm, controlled.

They were past him in a flash: such a pretty sight – breasts bobbing, eyes sparkling, the pair of long legs and the pair of short legs matched in rhythm as they snapped at the frosty ground. This was a story the children would want endlessly repeated – the story of how two beautiful girls ran a race for their father. And how the fittest, or luckiest, became their mother . . . The foolish smile remained on Gerald's lips. He was glad to be alone.

Just past Gerald, Rose slipped in a muddy patch of woodland track. She lost her footing for a moment. Recovering it, she saw Lola had increased her lead. For the first time, fear bristled through her, weakening her churning legs which, in wonderful response to all the training, had seemed till now prepared to pump on for ever. She knew that within half a mile they would be at the stream. Leap it, Gerald had said. Suddenly she quailed at the thought of leaping. She would slip, fall – something would go wrong. Better to run through it and risk being disqualified. The decision made, Rose put in a burst of speed. In a moment she was just behind Lola again: could hear her breathing and see dark shadows of sweat on the back of her tee-shirt.

At the stream quite a crowd had gathered. Rose heard cheering and more laughter. They were hollow, echoing noises. Mocking. Sharp with relish for an unusual sight. Rose hated their beaming, blurred faces.

Oh God, and now the stream. It looked so wide this

morning. Black water furred with melting ice and cracked sun. And suddenly, in an effortless leap, Lola was over it. *Racing up the bank the other side*. Increased cheers. Sickness in Rose's chest. She splashed into the water, felt the ice burn her calves, the mud slip beneath her feet. But somehow, then, she regained *terra firma*, clutching at clumps of prickly grass as she scrambled after Lola up the bank. Another cheer.

Upright again, her feet felt squelchy, soggy, heavy. It had been a foolish thing to do. It had lost her precious seconds.

Lola was ten yards ahead.

Lola had dry feet.

Lola would be Gerald's wife.

They were only halfway through the race, and already it was the end for Rose. Sad and angry tears blew from her eyes. She let them prickle down her burning cheeks. Spurred herself on, on. Maybe there was still a chance. Just in case, she could not give up trying.

Gerald's next position was the corner of a ploughed field. Two-thirds of the race over. Both girls tiring. Pace much slowed by the heavy black mud. Clothes and bodies darkly splattered, feet badly clogged. As they passed close to Gerald – Rose by now only just behind Lola, having made a remarkable recovery since her setback at the stream – Gerald could hear the duet of their breathing, and smell their sweat in the clear air. Irreverently, he was reminded of their different smells in other conditions. Poor girls, poor girls. In the warmth of his fleece-lined jacket, Gerald felt his heart expand with a strength of compassion that was strange to him. Well, he would make it up to them. One his wife, the other his friend. It would be all right. It was only light-hearted fun, after all, wasn't it?

Gerald turned to hurry along a short cut to the five-barred gates. These, he had stipulated, must be jumped or vaulted. If Lola cleared hers as easily as she had cleared the stream, the winner was in no doubt. Poor Rose. Dearly beloved Lola. Gerald felt for the flask of brandy in his pocket. He took a swig as he hurried towards his vantage point. A toast to them both, really. A toast of love.

* * *

Lola was less happy in the open. The winter shadows of the woods had been protective. Now, the expanse of opalescent sky pressed intimidatingly upon her head. Two worries concerned her: she had been constantly in the lead. That, surely, was a bad omen. And a quarter of a mile ahead was the five-barred gate. Years ago no gate could have daunted her. She had always been a good vaulter. Now, she felt the energy required to heave herself over seeping from her body. It seemed a terrible obstacle.

The sun, much stronger, was in her eyes. Her feet were heavy with mud from the plough. That had been a stupid idea of Gerald's, the plough – guaranteed to slow them both up. Just behind her she could hear Rose's heavy breath. They were running downhill, an easy field of cropped grass. At the bottom, the two gates were set side by side in the hedge. Lola was to take the right, Rose the left. They had decided that without telling Gerald. No doubt he was expecting to enjoy their confusion. Well, he would be disappointed.

Lola saw a large crowd at the gates, heard the braying laughter and cheering from well-scarfed throats. Damn them. They were waiting for a fall, disaster. She hoped neither she nor Rose would reward them.

After the gate, there was the short last lap up the steep hillside to the gibbet; and the final hundred yards down the sheer incline to the other side, to the winning post. So the race was nearly over. Lola was tired, but had reserves of energy. She increased her speed, enjoying the gentle downward slope of the field.

All too soon, the gate was before her. Jump or vault? Having made her decision, definitely to vault, it suddenly left her. The silly shouts of the spectators confused her. She sprang on to the top bar, swung her legs over her head – a perfect vault. But, regaining her feet, she saw that Rose was now ahead. The cheering had been for *her*: even as she concentrated on leaping the gate herself, Lola had been conscious of a perfect high jump by Rose over the other gate. Oh God, now there was fear. The sharp pull of the hill began almost at once, cruel to tired calf muscles. Lola felt a fresh shower of sweat spray from her pores, soaking her clothes. She heard herself panting, saw Rose's muddy bottom pumping easily up the hill.

She, Lola, then, was to be the friend.

Rose the wife.

Rose the winner.

Not possible, really. The sky was crumbling, the steep earth a blur. Glancing briefly at the summit of the Down, Lola saw the deathly arms of the black gibbet, the only unmoving things before her desperate eyes. With a strangled cry, she called upon the last of the energy coiling in her blood. Maybe there was still a chance. Just in case, she could not give up trying.

Dazed, Gerald watched the two small, dirty white back views struggling up the hill. Lola was catching up, but only slightly. From this distance, Rose seemed to have more bounce in her stride. Although Lola's long loping gait was suddenly consuming the hillside amazingly fast.

Gerald allowed himself a quick look at the gibbet, its *rigor mortis* arms embracing the sky. Then he hurried back to his car to drive round the foot of the hill to the winning post. He wished he had chosen another part of the Downs to end the race. There was something macabre, perhaps . . . But then he had always been puzzled by his own black humour. At this very moment, it brought tears to his eyes.

He stood at one end of his shabby old red silk tie which lay on the grass. The large crowd of spectators kept a respectful distance behind him. This side of the hill, the gibbet was no less menacing.

Moments. Eternal moments. Brief seconds – Gerald had no idea which they were. Then they appeared on the summit, his girls – two small dots, neck and neck. Lola had made a remarkable recovery. As if by some private agreement, the two of them ran simultaneously beneath the gibbet's high arms – Rose tiny on the left, Lola very tall on the right. They glanced at each other. Gerald could have sworn they smiled.

Through his binoculars he recognised the automatic movements of four tired legs out of control. As they sped down the slope Rose seemed entirely pink, only her mouth a deeper pink hole. Lola resembled a runaway Arab horse – great mane of hair free from its ribbon now, flying loose behind her – beautiful nostrils widely flared. Both made their final effort, and Lola of the longer legs was just ahead again.

His heart blasting his chest, Gerald concentrated on the last moments of this race, the magnificent way in which Lola was to win him. In his excitement his binoculars slipped. It was with his naked eye he saw the large stone embedded in the ground ahead of her. He tried to shout, to warn.

But no sound came from his throat. He heard the cheering behind him, muttered some kind of prayer. Lola increased her lead with a leap of triumph. Behind her, Rose let out a terrible cry.

Then Lola fell. Her body flung out on the ground like a length of pale material let down by the wind. Rose, unable to stop, flashed past her and over the winning ribbon.

Gerald saw the crowd rush towards Lola before he was able to move. He was aware that Rose sat on the ground some yards behind him, shoulders heaving, moaning slightly, head bowed into crossed arms. Rose the winner.

Ignoring her, Gerald moved up the slope towards Lola. Someone was running towards a parked car, face serious.

The crowd made way for Gerald.

'She fell over a bloody stone.'

'Someone should have checked the slope was clear.'

Lola lay head down, face turned to one side. Eyes shut. Deadly pale. Mud streaking down the whiteness of her. Beautiful hair tangled with sweat. A small trickle of blood, to match the winning post ribbon, trickling from her temple.

'Unconscious.'

'Probably something broken.'

'Someone's gone for an ambulance.'

'Bloody good sports, both of them.'

Gerald, on the ground beside her, laid his hand over her warm temple. He listened to the voices, said nothing.

'How is she?'

He looked up to see Rose on the ground beside him. Rose, warm and smelling of sweat and mud and life. Tears running silently from her eyes.

'Who knows?' said Gerald, and turned his attention back to Lola.

The ambulance came. It had difficulty negotiating the steep slope. Two men with impenetrable faces and red blankets lifted Lola gently on to a stretcher. Gerald wanted to ask if she was alive – he had not dared put his hand on her heart. He said nothing.

One of Lola's arms trailed down the side of the stretcher, unconscious fingers feeling the ground whose frosty sparkle had melted. The ambulance left, its tyres cutting deeply into the mud.

'Quick,' said Gerald.

He took Rose's hand, familiar and warm, in his, and hurried her to his car before the spectators could begin to question. They followed the ambulance to the hospital in silence. Passing The Bear, he could not help wondering what would now happen to the lunch he had ordered for the three of them. He recognised the weakness. Always, in a crisis, his mind flew unbidden to trivial matters as if for protection from the gravity of real circumstances.

In the Casualty waiting-room, beside Rose on a plastic chair, he noticed the pinkness of her skin had gone. She was pale. Trembling. He felt in his pocket for his flask of brandy. They both took large gulps, both managed small smiles.

'Here's to the winner, then,' said Gerald, roughly patting her muddy knee. 'It was a magnificent race . . . a lot of fun. As for Lola . . .'

'She'll be all right,' said Rose. 'Honestly. I know Lola. She's had plenty of falls in her time.'

Lola never regained consciousness. She died from an internal haemorrhage two days later. Some months after her death, Rose and Gerald were married: a very minor ceremony, little celebration. To begin with, events did not impair Rose's love for her husband, though after marriage he became in many ways a stranger. It was as if he was haunted constantly by the thought of Lola – which, of course, Rose understood. It was a feeling shared. But after a year or so, Rose's patience with her husband's melancholy broodings began to fade, and regret at having won the race consumed her life. She imagined what might have been: Lola the happy wife, herself the brave and –

60

eventually – contented friend. She stared at what was: life with a trophy she had thought she wanted – a balding, querulous man, old before his time, his charm quite flown. As she walked with him through the graveyard of stiff white stones Rose knew that he was empty of all thought of her, and only Lola, long bones in her grave, was alive in his mind.

Donkey Business

*T*he first day of the season, the donkeys were always hesitant. Ears pricked high, remembering the way, they walked close to the pavement, re-accustoming themselves to the sound of the traffic. Their nervousness would be gone within the week. For the moment, Jo, at the back of the line with his ash stick, encouraged them.

'Along there, Pat! Lulu, Oliver, Fancy, Skip. As for *you*, young Hasty!'

He brought the stick lightly down on Hasty's grey haunches. She was a good-tempered beast, but slow. Nothing could hurry her, or excite her. A bit like Jo's mother, in many ways, and Jo, who was a patient man, was fond of them both.

The only one to whom Jo gave no commands was Storm. A small, brown donkey, Storm was a natural leader: an animal of exceptional intelligence. As Jo often said, Storm could *think*. His instincts were always right. There was that time a silly woman insisted her screaming infant should have a ride. She put him on Storm's saddle. The child sobbed. Storm refused to budge. He listened unmoving to the noise for a while, then lay down on the sand. The child was able to dismount, and ran away gratefully. Jo would never forget that occasion. It was one of the many times Storm had shown wisdom and kindness.

He led the way, now, down the concrete slope to the sands. There, hooves sinking into the soft stuff for the first time in six months, he gave a small bray of pleasure, and broke into a trot. The others followed, eagerly. Jo ran behind them, the wind keen about his ears. When they reached the hard sand, washed by an early tide, the donkeys' hooves made a gentle puttering sound that Jo often remembered, but could never quite recapture, during the long winter months that he spent in the stables polishing the tack.

65

At an invisible point on the sand, precisely the right place, Storm came to a halt, turned his body parallel to the sea, and looked towards the far-off cliffs that edged the bay. The other donkeys copied. Unused to the spurt of exercise, their breath came bulbous from their grey muzzles, and they sniffed the raw smells of salt and seaweed in the air. They were all pleased to be back, Jo reckoned. Like him, they felt this was the life, down here on the beach.

Jo tucked his stick under his arm, put his hands in his large duffel pockets. Legs slung apart, he looked about the wide familiar territory of beach, sea, cliff, sky. The tide was far out. It had left a stubble of white foam drying on the ribbed sand. There was a whitish, cloudless sky that made the tracery of shadows very pale between the shallow mouldings of the beach. The coast, Jo liked to think, was gathering together its brighter colours to splash out in the summer months. Meantime, everything was nice and Aprilish – easy on the eyes.

It was too early in the year for anything but the rare customer. The crowds began mid-May, depending on the weather, but Jo didn't care. He liked it best when he had the beach to himself – just he and the donkeys. Then, he felt, privately, it was all theirs.

Jo had spent much of his thirty-two years on this beach with the donkeys. He knew no other life, desired no other life. His father had come from a long line of distinguished donkey breeders. He had died three years ago from a heart attack, while helping Lulu give birth to a stillborn foal. His mother, the daughter of a Punch and Judy man, had had hopes of being an actress. She settled, instead, for the chance to be Judy to her father's notorious Punch. From the dusky canvas box beneath the puppets' stage, she sent up a cacophony of Judy voices that soon became quite famous. Jo's father, as a young man in the audience, fell in love with the funny, raucous voices. He enticed the real Judy from the tent with the offer of free donkey rides, and married her at seventeen. They never left the northern resort where they met, and from his youngest days Jo remembered views of the bay from a donkey's back, two pricked ears spiking the huge blue sky.

Now that her husband was dead, Jo's mother over-worked herself in the small tobacconist's shop they had bought some years ago, to help pay the increasing bills for donkey food and bedding. For his part, Jo saw to the old stables that his father had built round the yard behind the shop. He spent every winter patching the roof, creosoting the weatherboarding, struggling to keep the rot at bay. But in his heart Jo knew that one day he would have to give up, and pull the buildings down. Their state of dilapidation was a great worry. But, away from them, on the beach, he could forget them.

He could forget everything, here, wind blowing a veil of sand on to his boots. It was hard to remember, even, what the skyline of the old town looked like before they built tall concrete hotels between the pretty Edwardian houses, that used to have the Front to themselves. Still, Jo was all for some change. So many people had come to the place last summer, attracted by the new holiday camp, the glassed-in swimming pool and the famous television comedian twice-nightly on the pier, that Jo's donkeys had made enough money to ease the winter months of no employment. Should be the same again this year. The long-range weather forecast had predicted a fair summer and, no matter what the state of their finances, parents could never resist donkey rides for the children.

Jo's reflections, practical rather than ambitious, were interrupted by a gentle bray from Storm. Most observant of donkeys, he had seen, before Jo, a figure in the distance. Jo screwed up his eyes. Seemed to be a woman: long skirts under a thick coat. Yes: definitely a woman. A small child walked at her side, holding her hand. Jo felt a fluttering of nervousness, as he always did with his first customer of the year. For she surely *was* a customer: she was approaching fast, now, eyes determinedly on the row of vacant donkeys.

Soon Jo saw her quite clearly: long hair billowing out to one side in the wind, bony face webbed with faint lines, surprisingly young grey eyes, pinkish cheeks but pale lips. A gypsy, most likely, Jo thought. It was too early for tourists, and local mothers never came down in the mornings.

She came right up to him, rather bold. The child clung to her dark skirts, burying its head in her side.

'How much?' she asked.

The question left Jo speechless. He had thought there would be several days in which to determine his rate for the year. He

67

had intended to think about the matter at leisure, fixing on a fair price which, while keeping pace with inflation, would not be so high as to restrict his customers' enjoyment. But he was blowed if he knew, at this moment, what that price should be. Eventually, fearing that the lady might grow impatient, he said, 'Off season rates, definitely.'

The lady nodded, smiling slightly, as if she didn't care at all what the off season rates amounted to. She patted Storm – they always patted Storm first – running a long white hand through the shaggy winter growth of his coat to where, Jo knew, she could feel the warm and softer fur beneath. The hand, curving through Storm's mane and down his shoulder, put Jo in mind of a fish: it was a graceful thing, somehow: gentle and slithery all at once. Not at all like the normal clumsy pat.

'You look like a bit of an expert,' he said.

'Oh, I'm used to animals, all right,' she answered. 'Can we take this one?'

Jo nodded. He knew she was the kind who'd like to lead Storm herself – not that Storm needed any leading. She swung the child on to the saddle with one skilful movement. Jo could see now it was a boy: curly flaxen hair, happy slanting eyes, huge grin.

'Mind if we just go to the farthest breakwater and back?'

The lady spoke so quietly Jo could hardly hear her words in the wind. 'Course he didn't mind. Delighted, he said to himself, to find such early custom. My pleasure, madam, he said to himself, because it would not be in his nature to say any such thing out loud.

It was his pleasure to watch the lady walk away in step with Storm, one hand on the donkey's neck. She was definitely no gypsy. Not with that voice, that walk. He watched till they were a tiny shape on the horizon. Then they turned. Slowly, they grew bigger, clearer, till they were life-size. The lady's grey eyes, though sad, looked quite pleased.

'Thank you,' she said, 'we enjoyed that. I'm sorry we've been so long. Must have been a good half-hour.'

It had seemed like minutes to Jo, their journey, but he did not disagree. The lady brought out a pile of coins from her pocket. She handed Jo a pound. He stepped back, shocked.

68

'It's nowhere like a pound, especially off season,' he said.

But she insisted. 'Go on. You've had a long winter, and I've got plenty of money – that's one thing I have got. Please take it.'

Having no idea how to argue with women, Jo took the money. He watched the lady lift her child from Storm's back. The boy's smile faded, on the ground, but he made no sound of protest.

'Goodbye, then,' said the lady, and, taking her child's hand, she turned away.

To Jo's surprise, she came again at the same time next day. The child made straight for Storm, and they went for the same long ride. While they were away, Jo determined to make some conversation on their return. His mother had taught him always to be polite to women and, out here, no one listening, it was easier to put away the shyness that gripped him, stealing his words, that came in crowded indoor places.

So, when they returned, Jo put a hand on Skip's saddle to steady himself, and said, 'You come from round these parts, then?'

The lady seemed to hesitate, rubbing at the fur between Storm's ears.

'No,' she said at last. 'I just have to be here for a while. And you?' She smiled at him politely.

'Me? I'm here always. I live here the whole year round.'

The lady swung the child down from the saddle, perhaps no longer interested. Where to go from here? Jo knew she would be off in a moment, if he didn't think of something.

'My name's Jo,' he said.

'Mine's Ida.' She was feeling in a pocket for the money.

'I live with my mother above the old tobacconist's by the church. We sell mostly souvenirs, now, what with the price of cigarettes. Ices in the summer . . .' He trailed off, confused by his own rush of words. Then added, '. . . and postcards.'

In the silence that followed, Ida gave him the most beautiful smile Jo had ever witnessed from any human creature, making him oblivious of the boniness of her face, only aware of the pretty puckering of skin round mouth and eyes. Wonderfully unnerved, he kneaded Skip's mane with his free hand.

'What you ought to do,' she said at last, 'is to have postcards

69

made *of the donkeys*. Each one separate. Then everyone who rides them would buy one. You'd make a fortune, I bet.'

The brilliance of her idea rendered Jo quite speechless. He stood a full minute in silent wonder at his luck in meeting anyone so inspired.

'That's a grand idea,' he said at last. 'Thanks.'

Ida shrugged. 'Oh, I'm always full of ideas. Usually, people don't do anything about them.'

Then, before Jo could protest, she slipped a pound into his lunch bag on Hasty's saddle, and hurried off.

Ida and her child came back every day after that: Jo lost count of how many days they came. He began to look forward to seeing her every morning and dreaded the day she might not turn up. But she was always punctual, never put off by rain or a cold wind. Sometimes, Jo would leave the rest of the donkeys and accompany her and the child – her son, David, he learned – as far as the breakwater and back. They didn't talk much on these occasions: Jo had no wish to appear inquisitive, and Ida was not one to offer up much information of her own accord.

Then one day – it must have been late May – Ida asked him if she could bring David to see the donkeys in their stables. Jo agreed at once, but the idea of her visit put him in a state of some agitation. He had never mentioned Ida to his mother, not knowing quite what to say. Once, he had been about to confide to her that this was the best spring he could ever remember, no particular reason – then he had thought better of the idea, and kept his silence.

Ida and David came to the stables early one evening. Jo's mother was out, so there was no fear of her discovering the visitors. Away from the wide spaces of the beach, Ida seemed to Jo taller, and nervous. He himself was in much the same state. Having come home early to give the yard a special clean, he was aware he smelled strongly of manure. But Ida did not seem to notice. She went from stall to stall with the child, stroking each donkey's muzzle, murmuring things Jo could not hear. When they reached Storm, the child flung its arms about the animal's shoulders.

'He's grown very fond of them,' said Ida.

70

Jo thought there was sadness in her voice, as if her son's affection could somehow be destroyed.

'Still, there's a while yet. Thank you for letting us come.'

She fetched the child and hurried off, as if fearful of being late for someone or something. When she had gone, the yard seemed empty as it had never been before, and Jo longed for the safety of the next morning on the beach, and all the comfort of their more familiar meetings.

Just a week later, long after dark, Jo was in the stables cleaning bridles by the light of his father's old oil lamp. He could not hope to improve the shine on the soft, gleaming leather which he polished every day. But it was something to take up the restlesness of his hands: he felt very awake, a little uneasy.

He looked up, saw Ida standing in the door. He had heard no footsteps in the yard. She was by herself, wearing a long grey cloak. With no child at her side, she seemed strangely alone.

'Sorry to disturb you,' she said, 'but we suddenly have to go tomorrow. I wouldn't have been able to come down to the beach, so I've come to say goodbye.'

The reins in Jo's hands turned to ice. He put down the bridle.

'Come on in, won't you?' he heard himself saying.

'I can't stay more than a moment.'

All the same, she moved nearer Jo. The flat light from the lamp illuminated silvery marks of dry salt beneath her eyes, reminding Jo of the crusts of waves left on the beach by a strong tide. So close, Ida smelt like the interior of the warm flower shop on the front where he went on Mothers' Day. Standing there, she blotted out the stables' own smells of manure and hay. Jo wanted to put his hand on her arm, just touch her for a moment, more than anything he'd ever wanted in his life.

'One thing, can I ask you?' she was saying. 'It's David. He's grown so fond of the donkeys. Storm particularly. I wonder if you'd let me buy him? We'd be a good home. I'd pay you anything, anything.'

She sounded quietly desperate. Jo scratched his head. The

71

desire to touch her had not diminished in all the confusion caused by her question.

'It wouldn't be a matter of money,' he said, to give himself time.

'I could send a trailer for him tomorrow morning.' She sounded oddly practical.

Jo stared at her. He thought of her small silent son David – his unhappiness without Storm. He thought of his own future without Storm. Well, he could always train one of the others to lead, he supposed. And somewhere in the jumble of conflicting feelings, Jo realised that if Ida owned Storm she would have a reminder, perhaps, of their days on the beach.

'That'd be all right, then,' he said at last. 'I'd like young David to have him.'

They made arrangements for transport. Jo refused any money. When he finally managed to persuade Ida that to give her the donkey would be his pleasure, she turned to go. Raising her fish-like hand to her mouth, she blew him a kiss in the semi-darkness. Then the fingers flew away in an arc, and disappeared beneath her cloak. Jo could think of nothing to say, and in silence watched her leave.

Some time later, when he had finished the bridle, he went to Storm's stable. The animal made a small welcoming noise. Jo remembered the night of his birth: a wicked night, thunder, lightning, rain through the roof, the lot. Now, running his hand down the black line of Storm's spine, came disquieting thoughts of the emptiness of tomorrow. But soon, because he had an orderly mind in which optimism swiftly followed upon melancholy, he began to imagine the summer ahead: the record crowds, the happy children, the sounds of sea and laughter – all the pleasures that Jo had learned come every year in the donkey business.

Sudden Dancer

'*T* here's not much point, far as I can see,' said Joan Cake, 'keeping on going to these things. With someone who can't dance, that is.'

'You enjoy yourself,' said Henry.

'I'd enjoy myself more if I could dance with my husband.'

'You enjoy the outings.'

'It's not the same.

'I couldn't get my feet to dance, no matter what.' Henry sighed.

He and Joan sat together on the late bus home, their bodies rolling slightly, used to the journey. They were splattered with rain. From the hem and neck of Joan's mackintosh sprouted frills of pink net. Her hair, piled up in meringue-like curls, was covered with a transparent plastic hat. Her mouth was down.

'I don't like to remind you,' she said with a small sniff, 'but when you've been champion at something, once, you don't like to have to retire before you're ready. You don't like to have retirement forced upon you.'

'You dance with plenty of others,' pointed out her husband. 'You're never wanting for partners.'

He took her arm, as the bus drew up at the stop. He liked to think the descent from the bus might deflect her train of thought.

'Not the same as having someone you can always rely on,' retorted Joan, stepping recklessly into a puddle and soaking the toes that pudged through the straps of her golden sandals. 'The last waltz, this evening. There was no one to do the last waltz with me, was there?'

'I knew that's what was getting you down.' Henry was sympathetic. 'Still, you had a lovely foxtrot, just before, you said.'

75

Home, glittering mackintoshes hung side by side in the narrow hall, Joan smoothed the skirt of her bulbous pink dress.

'Only three months till the Christmas Ball,' she said. 'That should be a big do, if it's anything like last year.'

'Certain to be,' agreed Henry, dread in his heart.

Joan straightened herself, punching the rhinestones on her bosom.

'If we never went to anther dance, it wouldn't make a mite of a difference to you,' she shouted. 'I shall have to think about a new dress.' She knew the last suggestion, at least, would provoke her mild husband: he hated the very idea of anything new in the way of dresses.

'That one's very nice,' he said, sadly scanning the mass of pink. 'It's always been my favourite.'

'Huh! Not for a Christmas party.'

She paused, suddenly feeling all the despair of being wasted: all afternoon setting her hair, ironing her dress, doing her face, and for what? For a disappointing evening dancing with dull old men, and now this late-night confrontation with a husband who did not know the meaning of the word appreciation.

'I wish you could *try*,' she said.

Henry coughed. He longed to go to bed. After a dance, this was always a long ordeal, what with the ungluing of the false eyelashes, and the stuffing of tissue paper between each layer of the pink net. He tried to be patient.

'There are some things a person can't bring himself to do,' he said. 'But I do try in other ways, don't I? To make up?'

Joan laughed nastily.

'Lots of things you think I want. Bringing in the coal – I'd bring in the coal. Beating the doormat – I'd beat the doormat. Clearing out the bird – I'd . . . None of the things I really want. All I want is just the one thing. I'll put the kettle on.' She turned and stomped off down the passage to the kitchen.

Confused by the outburst, Henry followed Joan, watched from the door while she slammed mugs down on the table. The rhinestones on her bodice glittered at him like a swarm of angry red eyes, as she pirouetted to the fridge for milk and foxtrotted towards the sugar.

'One day, perhaps, you'll give some serious thought to what I'm saying.'

76

'Oh, I will,' said Henry, and the great mercy was that as his wife cha-cha'd towards the kettle, an idea came to him.

On the walls of the studio Fred Astaire danced with Ginger Rogers: huge, blown-up photographs, a little muzzy, for the cameras of those days were not quite up to the speed of their twirling. Henry stood in the middle of the bare floor marvelling at the sight of them. His hand closed more tightly on the small paper bag that held his lunch. He listened to the thirties music that oozed from a small grille high up in one of the walls. He half-closed his eyes, felt himself spinning as fluently as Fred Astaire . . . Wonderful. Joan, light in his arms, smiling up at him.

When Henry looked down, eyes fully open, he saw he had raised one leg, slightly, but had not moved an inch. Fearful that he should be caught in so foolish a position in the middle of the floor, he hastened to a chair at the side of the room and took out his sandwich. A moment later Madame Lucille entered. Madame Lucille was well into her sixties, but you could see at once she had been a famous dancer in her time – the bouncy walk that set the muscles of her calves twinkling up and down.

She made an impressive entrance for Henry alone, coming right up to him before she spoke. She had white-blonde hair and powdered wrinkles. Her multi-coloured dress clung everywhere.

'Mr Cake?'

'That's right.'

'I'm sorry to have kept you waiting, Mr Cake.'

'No trouble.'

Madame Lucille's eyes jumped with great disdain to Henry's sandwich.

'Have you come here for your *lunch*, Mr Cake? Or to learn how to dance?'

'Oh, I'm so sorry. You see, it's my lunch hour. I thought a quick bite . . .'

'I'm afraid we cannot entertain eating and drinking in the studios, Mr Cake, though I'll close my eyes to it this once.'

'Thank you.'

77

He slid the sandwich into the pocket of his mackintosh, and laid the mackintosh on the chair.

'You'll have to make your appointments after work. On your way home. I'm open till seven.'

'I'm not sure I could work that in –'

'It's up to you. Now, shall we begin?'

Madame Lucille offered Mr Cake her hand, led him into the centre of the studio.

'What stage is it you're at, Mr Cake? As a dancer?'

'Oh, quite a beginner, I should say.'

'Then we shall start at the beginning.'

Henry felt a freezing sensation in his legs. The flesh of his hand that Madame Lucille clasped in her warm little fingers had turned entirely to bone. Anything to put off the moment when she would urge him to move . . .

'But my wife, she's a champion,' he said. 'She won cups all over the Midlands before we married.'

'My. Did she?'

'That's the trouble, really, with her being the champion. I didn't think it would be, but it turned out to be.'

'So you're here secretly – a few lessons – to surprise her?'

'How did you know?'

Madame Lucille smiled. 'Thirty years of secret plotting husbands, Mr Cake. I can tell the look in their eyes. I'm the heroine of many confidences. I've sent so many on their waltzing way, happy. Thirty years.'

'Oh.' Henry inwardly marvelled, already happier at the prospect that he might be added to her list of successes.

'Right. So, let's get down to it, shall we? We begin like this. By relaxing.' Her fingers loosened a little on his hand. 'What I'm going to do is to ask you to shut your eyes, to hold up your head, as if you were sniffing something nice, like spring in the air, and then let yourself feel the blood flowing right down through your body and into your feet.'

And just how does blood flow through bone, Henry wondered. He watched as Madame Lucille, close beside him, shut her eyes and sniffed. She seemed to be all puffed up, somehow, in a way that he could not imagine he would be able to imitate. She opened her eyes and looked at his feet. He felt his toes wince in the privacy of his shoes.

78

'So many beginners are frightened of their feet, Mr Cake. The first thing to learn is: they're nothing to be afraid of. You must learn to feel they're a part of you, *at one* with you. Not things you take off, like shoes.'

Madame Lucille had put into words something that Henry had suffered all the years of his marriage to Joan: fear of his feet. Now that the words had been said out loud he gave a small sigh of relief. The merest trace of courage quickened his stiff-boned body. He should have sought Madame Lucille's help years ago . . .

'Now, on with the dance,' she was saying. 'I think we'll start with the waltz.'

'My wife loves a waltz,' said Henry. 'The Blue Danube.'

'That's a fast waltz, Mr Cake. Lesson eight or nine, depending on progress. If you can be just a little bit patient . . .'

She took his hand again, and pointed her toe.

'Still raining?' asked Joan, when Henry arrived home.

'Pouring.'

'I haven't been out, what with my hair.'

She patted the rollers. Henry had never been quite able to accustom himself to the sight of his wife in rollers, but knowing they were necessary to the dazzling pyramid she concocted for nights out, it was a feeling he kept to himself.

'Anything untoward?'

Henry gave a small inward jump. Surely his face betrayed no trace of guilt?

'That's a funny word, for you.'

'I heard it on the radio. It appealed to me. You know I like to adopt new words. You know what I am for extending my vocabulary.'

Henry laughed.

'I love your sense of self-education,' he said.

'It's you who should have more sense of self-education. In some areas, I mean. The arts. Who cares about *gas*?' All their married life, Joan had scorned Henry's job with the Gas Board. 'There are some things any man who calls himself a man should know how to do.'

Henry sighed. 'Come on, Joan.'

79

'I've pressed your suit,' she said, lips pursed.

'What for?'

'Tonight.'

'What's happening tonight?'

'The do up at the Winter Gardens. Live band.'

'But I thought there was nothing else on this week?'

'Maybe it slipped my mind to tell you.' She paused. 'I could always go on my own, of course, if you didn't fancy coming.'

'Don't be daft,' Henry snorted. She had never made such an outrageous suggestion before in her life.

'I dare say I'd be all right. I wouldn't mind.'

'Well, I would. Letting my wife out alone at a glittering function.'

'My age, I don't suppose I'd be fighting off the rapists.' She watched her husband stiffen. 'It's all over by midnight.'

'There's no question of it.'

'It's quite inhibiting, sometimes, knowing you're there all the evening just watching.'

'But I don't watch with disapproval, do I? I'm happy to see you enjoying yourself. You know that.'

'You're always watching. I can feel your eyes right through my back.'

'I'm sorry. There's not much else I can do. Not much I have in common with dancing people . . . They all go there just to dance.' Something in his voice diverted Joan's attack.

'I'll take the entrance money out of the housekeeping if you like,' she said.

'Don't be ridiculous, love,' said Henry. 'I have the money.'

Some hours later Joan came downstairs in a foaming mass of lime tulle.

'You must be mad, thinking I'd let you out alone looking like that,' said Henry. Joan flipped his cheek with her lime glove.

'Sometimes, you know, I dream you're Henry Cake Astaire. Off we go, and when we get there you whirl me round all evening, keeping up the compliments in my ear!'

'Ah,' replied Henry, the bony feeling stiffening his limbs again. 'I've filled the log basket, laid the breakfast.'

80

In Joan's eyes he saw a sneer that pierced his heart.

'Come on, Fred,' she said.

To Henry, one dance hall was much like another. Each glittering function, as he had learned to call it, was identical in its crowd of elderly, over-dressed dancers dizzying their way about the floor to the old tunes of a tired band. He failed to see the glamour that enchanted his wife. Her eyes, as usual on arrival, swept about the place with an anticipation out of all proportion to the occasion, so thought Henry, privately. He suggested a drink.

'I haven't come here to drink,' snapped Joan.

'No need to look so frantic,' returned Henry.

Two nights out running and he found his normal reserves of understanding severely tried.

'I'm not looking frantic! And I wish you'd sit *down* somewhere, Henry. Nowhere near the dance floor.'

Her eyes swerved from her husband to a middle-aged man with crinkly hair who was approaching.

'What did I tell you?' said Henry. 'Here's Romeo.'

'May I have the pleasure?' the man asked Joan, for all the world as if Henry did not exist.

'Why, Jock,' smiled Joan warmly, 'I do believe we meet again.'

Henry watched them glide away, merge with the dancers, sway easily together, their feet in perfect harmony. He watched the crinkle-haired man, Jock, look down on his wife's careful curls, and smile. He remembered Madame Lucille's words at the end of that first, difficult lesson. He was plainly not a born dancer, she said. But with a lot of practice, maybe . . .

Henry took her advice and changed to longer lessons after work. At first, his progress was definitely slow. But in the fifth week he felt for the first time some small sense of achievement, when Madame Lucille accorded him her first praise.

'There's really a breakthrough, this evening, Mr Cake,' she said. 'We're really getting somewhere, now, don't you feel?'

81

'If you say so.'

'How about one more turn?' She fluttered her lashes.

'No. Really. I must be getting back. My wife'll be wondering.'

'Of course. Well, there's Thursday to look forward to, isn't there? I thought we might try a quickstep, Thursday. I think we should try to race ahead a little if you're going to be ready for the Christmas Ball.'

The Christmas Ball. Just seven weeks to go, the evening Henry had planned for his surprise. He hurried home, noticing with alarm the time. It went so quickly, dancing.

He arrived almost an hour late, somewhat flustered. At first, it didn't seem as if Joan had noticed.

'Do you know what a sissoo is?' she asked.

'No. Why? Should I?' He wondered if it was a guilty man.

'It's a valuable Indian timber tree.'

'Is it really? That's most interesting.'

Joan dug a fierce needle into a froth of chiffon, a pink that hurt Henry's eyes.

'I learned that today. Some magazine. I like to pick things up.'

'That's good.' Henry sighed. He could see the way things were going.

'I like to try, you see. To extend my accomplishments. Which is more than can be said for some of us.' She paused, took a pin from her mouth, leaned across the table, crushing the silk. 'And why are we so late tonight, Henry Cake?'

Henry glanced at the clock on the wall to give himself time.

'I'm sorry,' he said. 'The traffic. Terrible jams.'

'Forty-five minutes to be precise. Am I to believe there have been traffic jams every Tuesday and Thursday for the last five weeks, Henry?'

'Very curious, I must say – '

'Very curious indeed. Very curious, too, that you're such a bad liar. If you'd been more clever you wouldn't have met her on such regular nights. You'd have jumbled them up – '

'Met who?'

'Whoever she is. I don't know.'

Joan dug her needle more fiercely into the material. Henry heard himself laughing.

'You mean, you think I'm meeting a woman, having an association, just because of a few traffic jams? Oh, Joan. Oh, love. Would I ever? Have I ever looked at another woman?'

'Not as far as I know.' Joan sniffed, almost convinced. 'But it's never too late. All I'm saying is, you've had your head in the clouds these last weeks. Your mind seems to have been elsewhere. That's all I'm saying.'

'You're daft,' said Henry, his heart racing.

'Maybe,' said Joan. 'But I'm not a fool. After all these years, I know when there's something up with you.'

The awkward encounter that evening alerted Henry's sense of urgency. Joan's suspicions, once aroused, would be hard to quell. It was imperative Henry should take extra care in the future, so that he would not be forced to spoil his surprise in self-defence.

For several lessons he made sure he left punctually, despite Madame Lucille's pleading with him to do a few more turns 'on the house', and arrived home in time. Joan made no further mention of his imaginary girlfriend. But then came the evening of the second breakthrough: Henry mastered the reverse turn in the fast waltz. In his excitement, he twirled Madame Lucille round the studio till she was quite out of breath.

'*Beautiful dancing,*' she declared, when eventually he stopped and they stood, with arms about one another still, panting. Henry glanced at the clock. Ten minutes late.

'Madame Lucille. I must *rush.*' He made to leave her, but she clung to him.

'No need to go on calling me *Madame* Lucille, is there, Mr Cake? After so many lessons? After all, all I want is that *your wife* should be happy with your dancing, isn't it – Henry?'

Quite violently, Henry wrenched her hands from his shoulders, and fled the studio. But he was out of luck. His slight lateness did not go unobserved.

'It's which one of us?' asked Joan, in greeting. 'That's what I want to know. Which one of us is it to be? Her, the trollop, or

83

me? It's up to you. The choice is yours. Give one of us satisfaction, stop mucking about with us both. That's all I ask.'

'What's all this?' said Henry.

'Such innocence! The game's up now, that's what. You can't draw wool over my eyes any longer. I know when I've been made a fool of, and I know when the time's come to put a stop to it.'

'Let me explain –'

'You explained last time. The traffic. I almost believed you.'

'It wasn't the traffic this time. But I'm not having an association, I promise.' He looked at her face. 'I have to admit, there are reasons I've been late. But they're reasons that will benefit you in the end. Can you believe that? It's the truth, I promise.'

'Huh, I don't know what to believe, I'm sure.' The edge had gone from her anger. 'There's never been any of this secrecy business before. Double bluff, most likely. Still, if that's how you want it, that's fine with me. Because I've made my decision.' She paused, pursed her lips. Henry dared not ask her the question. 'Nothing lofty, mind,' she said at last. 'Just, things will be a little different. I'll go my way and you'll go yours. I shan't worry any more if you're kept late by traffic jams. You mustn't worry if I join my partner for a cigarette after we've had a dance.'

Henry sighed, nodded silently. With any luck, before all that sort of gallivanting came to anything, it would be the Christmas Ball, his chance, and dancing together happily ever after.

'How long till the Christmas Ball?' he asked.

Joan snorted. 'You can't butter me up like that! I know you're not interested. Three weeks. There's bound to be a lot of Charlestons, always a favourite at Christmas.'

Henry turned away, dejected. He had not reckoned on the Charlestons. Another hurdle . . . More overtime, more difficulties. But he would manage it somehow.

And he did. In three weeks he had mastered the art of the Charleston, much to Madame Lucille's surprise, and his own. His rendering was a little cautious, but foot-perfect. With confidence, Madame Lucille assured him, he would become more flamboyant, twirling his hands and giving little flicks of the head, just as she did.

On the afternoon of the Ball, Henry had his last lesson. For the first time in his working life, he had taken an afternoon off. (It was easier to lie to the Gas Board, he discovered, than to his wife.) It was also the last lesson of his course, and he felt quite sad. He had enjoyed the lessons. Judging by Madame Lucille's farewell, the feeling had been mutual.

'Not much potential, Henry, when you started,' she said, 'but you've come on surprisingly. Your wife will never believe her eyes. I wish you luck tonight. You're one of my successes.'

'Well, thank you for everything, Madame Lucille.' His hands were trapped in her small warm fingers. The Charleston still played through the grille.

'There are some pupils, my dear Henry, that stand out in the mind . . . years and years. If ever you want a little course in revision, I'd be only too delighted, on the house . . .' She gave him a peck on the cheek, and they parted.

On his way home Henry had not known the thrill of such anticipation for many years. In fact, he felt quite dizzy, a little peculiar. His legs ached from all the Charlestoning, his heart was thumping. Not wanting Joan to observe anything unusual in his appearance, he decided to slip into the pub at the end of their street, and have a single medicinal brandy. He needed strength, courage, calm.

The pub was crowded, it took a long time to be served. Then Henry drank slowly so that the brandy's effects would be beneficial rather than inebriating. What with one thing and another he found that, to his dismay, it was past seven by the time he left. Still, they weren't due to catch the bus till seven-thirty. Henry hurried down the street, knowing Joan would be fretting, waiting for him to do up her hooks and eyes.

Home, he found the house empty. No sign of Joan. A note on the kitchen table.

I've gone on early, it said. *Please don't follow me, I want to go to this Ball alone. Seeing as how things have been this past few weeks, I'm sure you'll understand.   P.S.   All the same, don't worry.*

Henry crumpled on to a chair at the table, sunk his head to his hands.

It took him a few moments to make his decision. He changed

85

quickly, ran for the bus, arrived at the dance hall soon after eight. It was already crowded, the ceiling strung with balloons, Christmas trees in the corner. All very pretty, the perfect setting to put his plan into action . . . But the beneficial effects of the brandy had worn off. His heart reverberated all through his body. His courage had quite gone.

Henry soon caught sight of Joan. She was waltzing with the crinkle-haired Jock, laughing. Henry decided to waylay her when the dance was over, and ask her for the next one. But when the music stopped, and she walked with Jock unknowingly towards her husband, something in her face made Henry abandon his plan. He hid behind a pillar, watching as they made their way to the bar.

Henry remained hidden, dodging from pillar to pillar, most of the evening. His eyes scarcely left his wife, dazzling as ever in some new dress of gold sequins. The strange thing was, although she was rarely off the floor, she did not seem to be entertaining her usual amount of partners. In fact, dance after dance, she stuck with Jock. It was no doubt he was a very good dancer, though Henry could see little charm in the red puffiness of his face and the greasy gleam of his crinkled hair. Still, it was the *dance*, not the *man*, that Joan went for, as she always said.

The first Charleston added to Henry's distress. His toes leapt in his shoes – what he would have given to show Joan how he could do it! – while he watched her and Jock, flushed and laughing and winking, as they kicked up their heels. When the music came to an end, Jock took a handkerchief from his pocket. Joan snatched it from him and with a sort of secret smile – or so it looked to Henry from his distant viewpoint – dabbed his sweating neck. Henry could bear no more. He left.

He sat in the silent empty kitchen brooding for many hours. It was almost three when Joan returned. She came bouncing in, humming, snapping on lights, and was none too pleased to see Henry.

'What on earth?' she said. 'There was no need to wait up for me.'

She took off her coat. Henry observed that the expanse of

chest above the gold sequins had a bruised, flushed look. And
there was something strange about her face – her mouth. It
was pale as first thing in the morning. The carefully painted
plum red had quite gone. He made no comment, rose from his
chair stiffly.

'Lovely dress,' he said. 'Nice evening?'

'Very pleasant, thank you. Someone said they saw you. I
said they must have been mistaken.'

'Quite. Got the last bus, did you?'

Joan looked at him. 'No. Missed it. Got a lift.'

'Oh, good. Wouldn't like to think of you so late, walking
. . .'

'I was all right, don't worry. I can look after myself. Now
I've broken the ice I can do it again. You won't need to come
any more. All it needed was to break the ice.'

She pranced over to the stove, began to make tea. The gold
sequins twinkled conspiratorially in the harsh electric light.
Henry would have done anything on earth to have been able
to have seen through their eyes, tonight: to know what she
had been doing, just how her evening had passed. He gripped
the back of a chair, spoke softly.

'Joanie, if I was to say . . . What if I was to say I could
dance?'

Joan laughed. She did not bother to turn round.

'Huh! I'd say that was a good one. I'd say I'd believe *that*
when I saw it. After all these years of stubbornness.'

'Well, I'm saying it,' went on Henry. 'I can dance.'

Joan turned to the table with two mugs of tea.

'It was quite easy, breaking the ice, when it came to it,' she
said again, as if she had not heard him.

'Would you like me to prove it to you? That what I'm saying
is true?'

Joan sat down. 'You do what you like, one way or the other.'

Henry left the room, went to the sitting-room, and put a
record on their old gramophone. 'The Very Thought of You.'
Back in the kitchen, the sound was very thin.

'There,' said Henry. 'Well, would you care to dance?'

'What's all this?' Joan wrinkled her nose. 'Be a bit silly, here
in the kitchen, wouldn't it?'

'If my plans had worked out, and you hadn't wanted to be

87

alone, we would have been dancing together at the Christmas Ball.'

'Likely story! So who's been teaching you to dance?'

'Come on. Give it a try.'

Joan stood, half reluctant, half intrigued. She stood with hands at her side, grasping bunches of sequins on her skirt.

'Not much room in here, is there? – '

'The heater's off in the front room.'

' – For you to show your paces.'

They were suddenly shy of each other.

'You could make allowances,' said Henry. He stepped towards her, nervous. Held her stiff arms. He waited for a bar or two, counting under his breath. Then they began to waltz, moving cautiously round the kitchen table.

'How'm I doing?' he asked after a while.

'Amazing.' Though Joan's feet responded naturally to the rhythm, her voice was flat. 'I would never have believed it.'

Henry laughed, tightening his grip on her golden waist.

'Thought I'd surprise you. I'll tell you all about it, one day. Those traffic jams.' More confident now, he twirled his wife more firmly. 'Dance with anyone special tonight, did you?'

'No. Well, the usuals.'

'Jock included?'

'One or two with him.'

'He's a lovely dancer, Jock. Brought you home, did he?'

'He lives this way,' said Joan.

'The very thought of you,' murmured the singer, making Joan shut her eyes with a small wince of pain that Henry did not see. Then the music changed to a quickstep. Henry was all delight.

'Hey! I can do this too, you know. I can do all sorts.'

But Joan was pulling away from him.

'Come on, Henry. That's enough. Tea's getting cold.'

'Just a minute more. I'm beginning to get the feel of it. Come on, Joanie, be a sport.' She ceased to struggle against him. They moved round the kitchen table once more. 'Tell me, honestly – am I any good as a dancer?'

'You're a lovely dancer.'

In his exuberance, Henry did not notice that Joan's voice was weary, and that her dancing, for all its accuracy, was

88

uninspired, automatic. 'Turns out, though, it isn't just the dancing that counts. Not just the dancing,' she sighed.

Henry, his head pressed excitingly close to her myriad curls, could not be sure what she said.

'What's that?'

'I said you're a lovely dancer, Henry. A lovely dancer.'

'Just think . . . years ahead. What you've always wanted. Me to dance with. How about that?'

With unbounded happiness, Henry twirled even faster, undaunted by the surprising heaviness of his wife in his arms. He tripped slightly in a reverse turn, but no matter. They both recovered together, Fred Astaire and Ginger Rogers, whirling through timeless space between kitchen table and stove.

'How about that, indeed,' answered Joan, seeing a grey dawn through the window.

Despite this sudden dancing, she was feeling the cold. She hoped to goodness Henry would soon be finished with his quickstepping, and let her have her cup of tea.

The Bull

*T*he bull had spent a restless night. Through the shallows of her sleep Rachel had heard him snarling and groaning, sometimes angry, sometimes sad. Now at dawn she peered through the curtain of the small window to look at him: he stood knee-high in mud, curly forehead stiffly silvered with frost, furious pink-lashed eyes staring at the cows on the far side of the field. Maddened by the way they ignored him, he roared again, a sound that ended in a high-pitched whine: a sound pathetically thin from so large an animal.

Rachel shivered and got back into bed. She wished Jack was there. But he was away on one of his conference trips, the Canary Isles this time. She had had a postcard saying wonderful sun for the time of year, and too much wine. He always sent her postcards but never said he missed her. Sometimes Rachel wondered how the evenings on such trips were spent. Jack often said they were very boring, endless talking shop at the bar with the boys, and Rachel liked to believe him. But occasionally the nastier part of her imagination activated itself, and she imagined her husband slapping his thigh in delight at strip shows, or flirting with a passing air hostess. She never, of course, spoke of her suspicions: they only came to her because her days were too empty. In their idyllic cottage, a mile from the nearest village, there was little for her to do: no defences with which to keep lurid thoughts from an empty mind. Every day she wished she had never agreed to leave London. But it was too late now. Nothing on earth would make Jack return.

The last time he had been home, ten days ago, Rachel had mentioned the bull's restlessness, wondering what it meant. Jack had laughed at her, seeing the unease in her face. He often scoffed at her for her lack of understanding of the countryside. When she could tell an elm from an ash, he said, he would take her fears seriously. As it was, the bull was like a frustrated old man – feeling sexy, but overweight and not up to it. No wonder he bellowed all night. Wouldn't anyone?

Rachel managed to laugh. Standing in the kitchen in his vast gumboots, Jack seemed very wise. When he was at home there was no worry that the bull, suddenly enraged, might trample over the flimsy fence that divided their garden from the field, and storm the cottage. When Jack was there, throwing huge logs with one hand into the fire, or tapping his pipe on the hearth, any such thoughts seemed absurd. When he had gone for a while, they came back to haunt her, and she made sure she never went into the garden wearing her red skirt.

Back in bed Rachel knew she would not be able to go to sleep again. She stretched a foot into Jack's cold part of the sheet, and wondered how she would pass the day. Squirrels in the roof scurried about: she tried to imagine the dark warmth of their nest, and felt grateful for their invisible companionship. At first, thinking they were rats, their noises had alarmed her. But now she was used to all the sounds of the cottage, the creaks when the central heating came on, the gurgle of pipes, the flutter of birds nesting in the eaves. Now, none of them alarmed her. Even on stormy nights alone, rain pelleting the windows, wind keening down the chimney, she was not afraid. She was only afraid of the bull.

Smiling at her own stupidity, Rachel got up and put on her dressing-gown. She went down to the kitchen and switched on the kettle. Outside, the morning was pale. A yellowy light, reflected in the water-logged field, meant a weak sun was rising. The distant cows, lying down, were almost submerged by mist. The bull stood up at the fence, chest rubbing against it. The wire bent beneath his weight. Rachel could hear the animal's soft, patient lowing. Hand curiously unsteady, she cut herself a piece of bread and put it in the toaster.

Then she looked at the bull, eye to eye. It jerked its head back, increasing the large folds of reddish skin round its neck. Its dilated nostrils smoked streams of warm breath. The small mean eyes remained on her face.

'Bugger you, bull,' said Rachel out loud.

There was a loud roar. Rachel jumped back from the

94

window. The bull moved away from the fence. Turning its back on the cottage it rumbled towards the cows, hunch-shouldered, long scrotum swinging undignified as a bag of laundry against its muddy hocks.

Rachel heard a click behind her. In her nervous state, she jumped again. It was the toast, blackened. Smoke filled the room. She opened the back door, felt a blast of cold air, watched the blue smoke seep on to the terrace. The bull had almost reached the cows by now. So far away, Rachel felt quite safe. The pomposity of his shape reassured her. If that bull had been a man, he would have been a chairman – a stumpy-legged, huge-bellied chairman, rolling down executive corridors chewing on a fat cigar. He would have been disliked, not trusted, but respected for his power. At office dances he would nudge secretaries with plump knee or elbow – even as now the bull nudged one of the cows which, in awe, heaved itself to its feet.

Rachel ate her breakfast at the kitchen table. She would begin the day, she decided, with a long bath. Then, in preparation for Jack's return at the weekend, she would defrost the fridge. The igloo appearance of the freezer, which some-how she never noticed, annoyed him on many occasions. He said she took no care of possessions. Their attitude to posses-sions was very different. Their attitude to most things, in fact, was rarely similar. For the hundredth time, that winter morn-ing, Rachel wondered why she had married Jack. Strange how you sometimes make major decisions without meaning to, she thought: strange how you bury your real will beneath a floss of superficial good reasons and act against your instinct. She had met Jack not long after her turbulent affair with the irresponsible David had ended. Exhausted by months of alter-nating hope and despair, she had in her weakened state settled for the promise of peace and security. They were assets she now regretted. It was danger, she had been forced to admit to herself, that she most relished. Without the possibility of danger her life lacked an element necessary to maintain her spirits. Often, these last, lonely months in the cottage, she found herself wishing for a fire, a burglary, a local drama – anything to menace the dull rhythm of her life.

Upstairs, after her bath, Rachel sat at her dressing-table

carefully making up her eyes in the way that had always pleased David. Sometimes she imagined that one day he would arrive, unannounced, to rescue her. She would not want to be caught looking less than her best. And so most days she made an effort with her appearance, in weary expectation.

She was thinking of David – the funny way his left cheek crinkled when he smiled – when she heard a crash downstairs. Then an almighty roar. Her skin shrank icily, pressing tightly over a wild heart. Glancing out of the window she saw the useless wire fence was flattened on the grass. She remembered she had not shut the back door.

With the speed of terror she ran downstairs and into the kitchen. The bull stood by the sink, its huge form blocking the door to the terrace. Beside it on the floor lay the smashed crockery it must have knocked off the draining board. Steam rose from its back, clouding a shaft of pale sunlight. It took a step forward, mud squelching from its hooves on the tiled floor. Then it raised its head to meet Rachel's look, and gave a deep noisy sigh.

For a moment Rachel was hypnotised into silence. For a moment incredulity overcame her: perhaps this monster in her kitchen was but an hallucination sprung from a despairing mind. The whole room caved about her, the thick stone walls suddenly no protection. All the familiar objects – china, dried flowers, candlesticks, basket of eggs – cracked in their vulner- ability. The bull growled. It was no illusion. Rachel screamed.

She fled, slamming the door behind her. But even as she ran to the telephone in the hall she knew it had not closed. With useless fingers she stumbled through the telephone book for the farmer's number. When the ringing was answered by an unknown voice she shouted an almost incoherent message. She could hear the bull whining and snorting in the kitchen. With great effort of will, as she slammed down the receiver, she forced herself to turn round. The bull had nudged open the kitchen door, was surveying her with malicious intent. It stamped a fore-foot. Mud on the pale carpet. Rachel screamed again.

She ran to the sitting-room, snatched up the poker. While one part of her terrified mind told her to run up the back stairs and lock herself in the safety of the bathroom, another, more reckless part urged her to fight the bull, to protect her possessions. Suddenly, for the first time, they seemed important.

Waving the poker she now approached the animal, shouting obscene threats. Confused, it backed away from her, until it was wholly in the kitchen once more. Rachel was sparked with the adrenalin of courage: with no thought for the foolishness of the action, she struck the bull on the nose. It gave an agonised roar and lowered its swinging head. One of its horns hit the television on the dresser. The screen splintered, cracking the small reflections of the quiet day outside. Further angered, the bull moaned again, prepared to charge. But its muddy hooves skidded on the polished tiles. Its knees buckled. It fell.

Rachel took her chance. She dashed past it, hitting it again on the nose. She dived for cover under the kitchen table, peered through the legs of the chairs, shouting all the time.

The bull, infuriated by its own foolish position, managed with difficulty to get up. It then spun round with astonishing dexterity and lowered its head towards the chairs that were Rachel's only protection. Snorting, it banged one with its head, sent it crashing to the floor. Then, seeing that Rachel was out of easy reach, it turned its revenge on the television set. One butt, and it smashed to the ground. China eggs, a jug of leaves, fruit, followed, different-shaped noises piercing the bull's now constant roaring.

From her position under the table Rachel watched the bull's campaign of destruction. She saw in close-up its spongy hooves slide in the mess of egg yolk and mud. She saw the dark matted hair of its belly and knees as it slid about in monstrous fashion, slashing at everything with its head. But by now all fear had left Rachel. With only the small risk of the bull reaching her, its livid roaring and thrashing thrilled rather than terrified. At last an outside force was smashing up her life. Here was reason to go. The brief protective feeling towards her possessions had disappeared. For all she cared, the bull could destroy as much as it liked. When, all too soon, she heard voices, and saw two farm labourers enter the back door, armed with pitch forks, she felt the chill of anti-climax.

The men's appearance calmed the bull, or perhaps its rage was already spent. Willingly it allowed itself to be led by the

97

ring in its nose on to the terrace, and back over the fallen fence into the field. The men were full of apologies and concern: the farmer was coming over at once, they said, to see about the damage. But the damage, for the moment, was of no concern to Rachel. Clearing up her shattered kitchen would nicely fill the days until Jack came home, then, with the weight of good reason on her side, she would make her announcement.

The men set about mending the fence. It would be replaced later in the day with a stronger one, they said. No need, Rachel replied: the bull's curiosity is sated. He wouldn't attack again. They chuckled knowingly, and said you can never trust a bull. It was pointless to argue. With a sense of real purpose – a strange and unfamiliar sensation – Rachel set about the long task of clearing up the mess.

When Jack came home two days later Rachel patiently listened to his week in the Canaries before telling the story of the bull.

Consumed by his own dreary tales of seven innocent evenings of drinking at the hotel bar, he failed to notice the television set was missing, as were many pieces of china and other objects long established in their place on the dresser and shelves. When Rachel told him what had happened, he was incredulous and concerned. His concern, however, was not so vital as to cause him to suggest a change of life. No: he merely guaranteed he would assess the strength of the new fence himself, and have some pretty sharp words with the farmer about damages. Rachel mustn't be frightened in future: it would never happen again, he could assure her.

In return Rachel assured Jack she would certainly feel no fear in the future, because she would be far away. She was leaving him. There was no point in Jack making promises for the future, or trying to persuade her to stay. It would be a waste of breath. Her mind was made up. Also, as it would be pointless to spend the weekend together, she would be grateful if he would run her to the station in the car. She would leave her own car behind and go by train to London. She had no idea where she was going. She would make up her mind on the train.

Seeing the seriousness of her intent, and knowing she would change her mind in a few days' time when the reactions of her nasty experience had spent themselves, Jack, with a small secret smile, obligingly took her to the station. He handed her the suitcase – rather a large one, admittedly, but then she had to play out her silly game to the full, of course – in a friendly manner, and kissed her on the cheek. As for his part, he congratulated himself on playing it impeccably. He said he would send extra money to their joint bank account, and Rachel should feel free to draw on it as she wished. Driving back to the empty cottage he felt full of understanding. Rachel had always thrived on a bit of drama: perhaps in future when this silly incident was over, he would try to provide a few more excitements in her life. What an effort, though: the price of not having married a peace-loving wife, as he had always intended, after all. Ah, well. He looked forward to a quiet evening by the fire.

Rachel arrived at Paddington just before midnight. She lugged her suitcase to the taxi rank. Before she had time to think – which she had resisted doing on the train – a taxi appeared. The driver asked where she wanted to go.

Rachel had not been in London for a long time. It was too late at night to arrive on the doorstep of friends she had not seen for many months. There was only one place she could be certain of being received with real pleasure, wasn't there? She gave David's address.

David had said so often he would always love her. They had not communicated for nearly a year, but that would not change things, surely. He was a man who kept his word. She did not doubt he would be alone: he was not the sort of character who would replace his women in a hurry. Rachel was certain he would be pleased to see her again, for all the ugliness of their parting.

No: it wouldn't be too late, she was sure. But as the taxi sped through the empty streets towards his house, Rachel felt the thrill of fear again, the snarl of danger in her bones. She was reminded of the bull – its rage spurring her own excitement and fear. She felt grateful to it for rousing her from an apathy which had gripped her for far too long. Had it not been for the bull's attack, she would never have been here, now, boldly returning to her old lover with no idea of what kind of future awaited her. As the taxi drew up at David's house – a light on in his bedroom – for one last moment Rachel imagined Jack, alone in the kitchen at home, smoking his pipe by the fire, listening to the roar of the bull outside. Smiling to herself at the thought, she rang David's bell and waited.

Balloons

At eleven-thirty the night before Timothy's party, Catherine was still blowing up balloons. The ones she had already finished, all colours and shapes, drifted slightly about the room, pushed by a breeze from the open window.

It was a mild night for October. Catherine felt hot, and her head ached from all the blowing. She had not bothered about dinner, so was also hungry. Some of her friends threw themselves gleefully into preparations for their children's parties, she reflected, and she wished she was one of them. But she found the whole thing a great effort, and worried for weeks about the birthday cake and expensive bags of going-home presents and the bloody balloons . . . The fact that Timothy's friends always enjoyed themselves made no difference to her annual anxiety. Still, this time tomorrow the whole thing would be over.

Seven, she thought. Timothy. Seven years ago. Unbelievable. The passing of every year, in middle age, grows more unbelievable.

Catherine picked up the last yellow balloon and blew into it with a final effort. Her head cracked with renewed pain. To hell with it. There were quite enough. She let it wither back into her hand with a little snorting noise. It lay there, a deflated caterpillar, slightly warm. And where was Oliver? Unlike him to be so late, knowing he was needed to help. He had a tedious amount of evening meetings and dinners, since he had been made managing director, but was rarely very late. Catherine felt a surge of annoyance. He knew what she was like about parties, what a nervous state they caused her. He knew she would have wanted his support this evening, though, of course, he could not know what sort of day she had had – a flat tyre, the dentist, four shops to find white candles . . . and just very tired.

But there he was, the familiar bang on the door. He hurried in, carrying a huge parcel.

'Timothy's train set,' he said. 'I managed to get it just before they closed.'

'Wonderful,' said Catherine.

His sudden presence demolished in a trice the resentment that had built within her.

'I'll wrap it up in a moment. I've written a card. You'd better sign it, though he won't bother to read it.'

Oliver was pouring two glasses of whisky. 'I'd rather thought it was *my* present, actually,' he said, throwing ice carelessly into the glasses. 'I mean, it was my idea. I found it. I paid.' He turned, watched the incomprehension shift across his wife's face. 'Oh, all right, then. It'd better be from us both.' He passed Catherine a glass.

'Well, our big present is always between us, isn't it? Thank you.'

Oliver sat in his usual chair by the fire. He gave a small kick to a couple of balloons at his feet, watched them jump along the carpet.

'You've been hard at work,' he said. 'Everything under control?'

A small pulse ticked in his neck. Catherine stared at it, fascinated. She had never seen it before.

'I think so,' she said. 'I picked up the cake, a pretty good chocolate engine, though goodness knows what the sponge will be like. I had a bit of trouble getting the right candles . . .'

Catherine cut short this story, knowing it was the kind of event in her day that would not interest Oliver and for which she could expect no sympathy.

'There are still the strings to put on the balloons, but I'll do that in the morning and hang them about the place. Timothy insisted I wasn't mean with the balloons. Well, I haven't been, have I?'

She allowed herself a tiny smile of self-congratulation to make up for Oliver's indifference. He did not smile back. Catherine had learned long ago that efficiency in domestic matters was not the way to his heart, though inefficiency provoked his displeasure. No: he was a man whose objects of admiration were set on higher things, and she had come to accept that in this he would never change.

'But I must admit,' she heard herself saying, 'I could have done with a bit of help blowing them up. They're so *hard*, these days.'

'Sorry I was late.'

Oliver held his glass in both hands, looking down into the liquid as if studying a magician's magic ball. His fine, soft face, in this light, scarcely seemed to have changed in the fifteen years they had known each other, thought Catherine. Their eyes met.

'I'm leaving you, Cathy,' he was saying. 'I'm terribly sorry, but I'm going.'

As when a limb is broken in an accident, or an icy snowball breaks on warm skin, and there is no pain, no feeling, no immediate reaction of what is taking place, so all sensation but incredulity drained from Catherine. She stared at her husband, unblinking.

'What about Timothy's party?' she said at last. 'Leaving for where? You can't let Tim down like that, whatever the business.'

'Oh, the party. I'll be there for *that*. But you don't seem to have understood. I'm not going anywhere on business. I'm leaving for good. Leaving you and Tim, this house, our life. Finally going. Do you realise what I'm saying?'

'No,' said Catherine.

'How can I make myself more clear?' Oliver was trying to curb a flash of impatience. 'I'm *going*. For good.'

Catherine felt her hand freeze on her glass. She looked at it. The fingers swelled up and quavered, like fingers seen through a distorting mirror that makes you laugh. Her mouth, when she opened it to speak, puckered and trembled against her teeth.

'What have I done?' she asked.

'Nothing. At least, nothing I can really complain of. You've been a good wife to me in so many ways. That's been part of the trouble, the reason I've taken so long in deciding. That's what makes it so difficult a decision.'

'Difficult,' repeated Catherine.

The reality was beginning to seep through now, chilling her veins. In the blind alley of her mind she struggled to formulate another looming question.

'Why, then?' she asked.

Oliver gave a small shrug, an awkward smile. 'I can't lie to you. Another woman. I fell in love with her four years ago. I did try very hard, I promise you, to resist – '

'*Four years ago?* I don't believe it!' Catherine was on her feet now, scarlet and shouting. 'You've been deceiving me with someone else for four years? I don't believe it! Four years of no clues, no hints, carrying on being so ordinary to me, same as ever, loving, happy, I thought. It's not possible!'

'These things happen,' began Oliver. 'And stop shouting, or you'll wake Timothy.'

'Why do they happen? They don't have to happen if you don't want them to happen. You could have stopped – '

'I tried to at first. Very hard. In the end I didn't want to any more.'

He was quite flushed. A wisp of hair stuck out behind one ear. For the first time in her life, it occurred to Catherine that her handsome husband looked absurd.

'I see,' she said.

In the long silence that followed, she looked about her, at the familiar room made unfamiliar by the bright balloons shuffling about, drowning her in her own house. Glancing in the looking-glass above the fire, she saw her wracked face, and was horrified: in middle age, shock or great despair are brutal to unfirm faces – she had seen the quivering of troubled flesh on others' jowls, hated her own lack of demeanour. She knew her appearance would do nothing to endear her to Oliver, either. She sat down again, needing the steady hug of a chair.

'I always thought,' she said, 'we were absolutely all right, you and me, Ol. So many friends breaking up, but you and me . . . We've always said how lucky we are, haven't we?'

'Well, we were. We've had good years, I don't deny that.'

Another silence. I can't believe this, Catherine repeated to herself. Then eventually, she said, very quietly, 'This is madness, isn't it? Insanity. It's not true. It's not happening. We're going to wake up in a moment from this nightmare.'

'It's no nightmare,' said Oliver, curtly, 'though I can under-stand your shock. But didn't it ever occur to you that things hadn't been well, how shall I put it, quite *tickety-boo* for some years?'

Anger flamed through Catherine's spine. She sat bolt upright, knew she was going to answer.

'No! It did not occur to me things weren't quite *tickety-boo*, I'm afraid.' Ammunition fired, she slumped back, weak again. 'Does anyone else know?'

'I've not told anyone.'

'Thank God for that.'

'Do you want to know anything about it?'

'I suppose I'd better know the briefest outline. You could spare me the details.'

Oliver got up to fetch the bottle of whisky. As Catherine watched the man whom she had loved without reserve for fifteen years, memories of things innocent at the time began to bite. Last summer in Brittany, he had gone every day to the hotel to make 'business' calls, saying there was a crisis. There was an unexplained tie in his cupboard: he did not usually buy himself clothes of any kind. The trappings of infidelity, discov-ered in retrospect, are infinite in their cruelty. She accepted more whisky.

'We might have gone on for another thirty years, you and me,' Oliver was saying. 'That would have been perfectly possible. We could have carried on in our minor key of compatibility, if that's what it was, ignoring the constraints, the general lack of – '

'Constraints?'

'Yes, constraints. Is that a surprise to you? Had you no idea there were constraints between us? We could have ridden them, perhaps, had it not been for Jennifer – '

'*Jennifer?* God, what a name.' Catherine's voice rose: Oliver's fell.

'Jennifer made me realise that for the first time in my life there need be no constraints between two people, however difficult circumstances may be. She made me realise something I'd been trying not to observe since the early days of our marriage.' He paused to drink.

'What was that?' Catherine was relieved to find actual words could still be formulated, albeit shakily.

'She made me realise that though you and I were always very *companionable*, we were never at one in heart and spirit, never loved in a way that I now know – '

'Stop, Oliver. Such justifications are rubbish. I don't want to hear them.'

Companionable, merely? What could he mean? All the years of laughter, the marvellous spartan holiday in their Scottish croft, the daily, mutual pleasure of Timothy, the wild enchanting nights, often better now, even, than in the beginning? Only last week . . .

'I would describe our marriage as more than just companionable,' she said at last.

'That's the difficulty, when two people see the same situation in completely different lights. It's a hard fact, but what you may have seen as a loving, satisfying marriage, I've known for years, for *me*, was just . . . as I said. Ultimately unsatisfying, not what I wanted.'

This is *laceration*, thought Catherine.

'You bastard,' she said. And instantly regretted it. There was no point in returning insults. 'You can't just ditch me with no explanation,' she added. 'I want to know – '

'I've been trying to tell you. But I don't think this is the time to go over it all again.'

He glanced at his watch like an impatient doctor who had to deal with a tiresome patient. Catherine recognised his voice as the mildly firm one he employed if she suggested they should ask some of her old school friends, with whom he had nothing in common, to dinner.

'But perhaps you'd be interested to know that Jennifer is over, now. *Over*. Four or five months ago.' He gave a wry smile. 'So there's currently no one else. I'm not leaving you for anyone else, understand?'

'So much for unconstrained love,' said Catherine, unable to resist. 'Is that meant to be better or worse, leaving me for no one?'

'I don't know,' Oliver sighed. 'I've put it all in my solicitor's hands,' he went on quietly. 'I promise arrangements will be

108

amicable, fair. You and Timothy can stay here, of course. You won't be short of money.'

The rich divorcee, Catherine thought.

'What a funny time to tell me all this,' she said.

'I spent a lot of time trying to work out the right moment.' Oliver sounded almost boastful. 'It seemed to me – I mean, I imagined that with so much to do tomorrow it would take your mind off it . . . It was as good a time as any, I reckoned.'

Catherine tried to laugh. The result was more like a howl. Oliver, ignoring the savage noise, shut the window and switched off the lights.

'Bed,' he said.

Catherine stood up. 'I've a right to fight for you,' she said.

'Fight all you like. Nothing will change my mind. I've been weighing it all up for months.'

'You might have shared your calculations.'

'No point. As I said, my decision was nothing to do with you, fundamentally. Now, come on. Finish your drink.'

Catherine obeyed. She asked if she should make up the bed in Oliver's dressing-room?

'I'd rather you didn't. Unless you feel . . .' He seemed surprised she should suggest such a thing.

'I don't feel anything,' said Catherine. 'Except a little drunk.'

By the light from the hall, they made their way across the darkened room, kicking at the impeding balloons – some globular, some giant sausages, others decapitated heads with painted grins and pointed ears.

'Damn these things,' grunted Oliver, kicking. One burst with a squawk.

'Oh no,' groaned Catherine. She envisaged them all bursting, firing their irregular bangs like the guns of battle. How could she face Timothy tomorrow, balloonless?

But there were no more bangs. Oliver was careful. And in bed he held his wife in his arms as usual. She quivered, tearless.

'Whatever does it mean, this sudden hardening of your heart?' she whispered. It was easier to ask such a question in bed.

'I don't know,' he answered, and she could feel him,

strangely, wanting her. 'But I'm sorry. You must be brave. You're always brave.'

Oliver forgot to sign the card on Timothy's present, but Timothy did not notice, as Catherine had predicted. He was delighted by the train set, and other presents, spreading them all over the breakfast table. As for Oliver, except for a firmer set of his face, perhaps, a slight tightening of the handsome mouth (both changes so slight that none but a wife would notice them) he appeared completely normal, quite cheerful. Admiration of the presents delayed them. There was a sudden hurry to get ready, all the scatty urgency of late departure . . . Barely time for Catherine to straighten Timothy's tie, kiss her husband on the cheek.

'Back soon as I can for the party,' he promised.

Alone in the house, Catherine decided to take Oliver's advice and be brave. She set about her preparations with exhilaration surprising after the sleepless night. In the kitchen she cut sandwiches, mashed bananas, made biscuits into patterns on plates, mixed jugs of fruit cup and stuck seven infirm candles into the chocolate engine. In the sitting-room she pushed back the sofas to clear a space for Zsa, the charming post-graduate conjuror, who supplemented his days of research by entertaining children with his off-beat magic and childlike jokes. It would probably be the last such party, Catherine thought. Next year, at eight, Timothy would want some sort of sophisticated outing to McDonald's or a theatre.

The balloons seemed to follow her everywhere. In the dining-room they clustered round her legs as she carefully laid the table. She put cat masks at twelve places, piled up crackers, laid folded paper napkins printed with tigers on paper plates bright with matching tigers, and stuck striped straws into scarlet paper cups. Companionable, *companionable*? Very companionable, she and Oliver. The words rattled about like spilled marbles among the decorations, but they did not hurt.

Last job was to tie strings on the dozens of balloons. Catherine hung them in great clumps on the bannisters, over pictures, on the hatstand in the hall, remembering to reserve three for the front gate – universal signal of a party. Who on earth chooses the colours of balloons, she wondered? The sour reds, scorched oranges, raw yellows and chemical greens hurt her eyes. There were so many ugly colours in the commercial world. She had once asked Oliver if he was offended by these millions of hideous colours, in shops and towns, that confront us every day. He said no, of course not, and thank goodness he did not suffer from her over-sensitivity.

Companionable, companionable. The balloons all in place at last, never quite still, Catherine returned to the chair in which last night she had received the news of her husband's departure. The scene, so mad, so painful, so bleak, swirled like minuscule grains in her head. The far past she always saw in much reduced size (last night now felt like the far past) thus making its reality hard to vouch for. As for the present, this silence before the revelries, normality only blotched by balloons – what now? Should Oliver really go, sweeping familiar companionableness from her – what then?

Then, of course, life would go on. Different life with different possibilities. New challenges, new emptiness. But perhaps new rewards, too. Possibly even some kind of new love – the kind Oliver had found with Jennifer, and imagined he might find again. Perhaps it wouldn't be too bad, once she had grown accustomed to unmarried life. – It would also be inconceivable.

After a while, Catherine roused herself from her brief reflections, stood. It was time to brush her hair, pin on a brooch and a smile, be ready to welcome Timothy home shortly. She must check he had a clean shirt. She must plan how to approach Oliver tonight. She must continue to be brave, whichever way things went. Catherine smiled to herself. The trouble with good mothers, she thought, was that no matter the traumas in their own lives, there was simply no *time* to collapse.

It was an uproarious success, as always, Timothy's party. Twelve boys jerked shrieking through the rooms caught in a sleet of wrapping paper and ribbon, bursting balloons and upsetting books, ashtrays, lamps – but you couldn't put *everything* away, Catherine decided, every year.

Oliver arrived halfway through tea, which was devoured in a very few minutes. (Catherine had wrongly allowed fifteen.) The cake cutting was a ceremony made deafening with witches' screeches. The out-of-tune rendering of Happy Birthday made Timothy blush. Oliver smiled, helped his son cut the chocolate engine. Tea over, Timothy gave Catherine a sudden hug for no apparent reason. Her eyes stung. She felt the letters of the word *companionable*, sharp as beads, fetter her limbs, strangling. But at least for these two hilarious hours, as for the rest of the day, there had been little time for thought. Oliver had been right, as usual.

During the conjuror's masterful performance of cracking eggs and mixing them to a disgusting mess in a bowler hat while the children screamed their appreciation, Oliver, Catherine saw, eyed her with something like respect. Well, she had remembered to cover the carpet where Zsa performed with newspaper. Oliver always admired such forethought, expected it of his wife.

They were gone – parents with impatient eyes, minds on the rush hour: boys with their single balloon and plastic party-bags of sweets and water pistols. Timothy was finally in bed, the relics of his seventh birthday scattered on stairs, floors, chairs and tables. Catherine found a tray, went to the dining-room to clear the demolished tea that had taken so long to arrange. Crossing the hall, she found Oliver contemplating the bunch of unburst balloons still tied to the bannister. He held a pointed kitchen knife.

'Tim'll be glad there are so many over,' said Catherine.

She wanted to clear up fast, concentrate on the chicken Kiev for dinner, think about the proper discussion which must take place.

'I hate the things,' said Oliver.

Catherine continued on her way to the dining-room. As she scraped chocolate cake from plates, she heard a succession of quick bangs. She counted. Ten. Perhaps Oliver was going through a mid-life crisis, she thought, gripping the table to stop herself shouting. That must be the explanation for his curious behaviour of the last twenty-four hours. The male menopause, of course. Must be dealt with gently. She'd read enough articles about it. Catherine picked up a forgotten cat mask, licked jam from its nose, and put it on. Then a purple paper crown. Male menopause being the explanation, the first thing to do would be to make Oliver laugh. She'd always been able to do that, at least.

There was a final bang. Louder. The front door.

Masked, purple crown askew, Catherine carried the tea-tray to the front hall. The bunch of balloons was now a bunch of rubber ribbons hanging limply from their strings. Life, tension, air, gone from them. Unable to chase her any more. Next year, she would get one of those pumps to blow them up . . . no need for the chicken Kiev, now, was there?

Catherine moved automatically to the kitchen, set down the tray, vision impaired by the cat mask. Perhaps, though, she should still cook it. It was more than likely Oliver had just gone down the road for more cigarettes. Scraping the parsnips would give her time to think. Calmly, rationally. The party over – and, heavens, it had been a good party, Timothy had loved it – her mind uncluttered at last, she could work out whether this little *fracas* was serious, and Oliver meant all he had said last night. Or whether it was merely one of those moods of no importance that sometimes come to ruffle even the most companionable of marriages.

A Matter of Diplomacy

*F*rederick, who by now was quite inured to Lizzie's looks of hopeful anticipation, decided to take matters into his own hands and surprise her when she least expected it.

They were standing around in Lizzie's small sitting-room, drinking glasses of sherry in front of the spitting gas fire. Frederick did not like sherry, as Lizzie well knew. But she considered a choice of drinks, at this point in their affair, a luxury she could not afford. Cautious by nature, she could not bring herself to invest in so much as a bottle of whisky until she knew the chances of permanency were high. But a full tray of every drink a man could desire was the promise she held before Frederick: her frequent hints as to her future generosity, should things 'change' between them, were not lost on her lover. He pondered upon them sometimes, when there was nothing else to occupy his mind, and wondered if, even accompanied by a galaxy of whiskys and gins, she was the girl for him.

This evening was to be as many other evenings: an argument about parking, a film, another argument about parking, dinner in a cheap Turkish restaurant, and a final argument about in whose flat they should spend the night.

The drinking of the abominable sherry was the lull before the friction, and Frederick took advantage of it to break the news.

'I've been thinking,' he said, 'of sending round my sideboard. How does the idea appeal?' With a vague wave of his free hand, he indicated the stretch of wall between gas fire and corner, only occupied by a nasty early sixties chair with spindle legs.

Lizzie, stunned by all the implications of the question, could not answer for some while. It was a funny way to approach

Matters, she thought, but then Freddie always had his own style of doing things. And if he cared to send his sideboard on ahead, before moving the rest of his effects and himself – that was fine with her.

'You mean *here* – there?' she said at last, following his gaze.

'There. Precisely.'

'Would it fit, Freddie? Wouldn't it be too long?'

'By my calculations, it would fit very nicely.'

'And of course it would be useful. I mean, I – we – could put things on it, couldn't we?'

'Quite,' said Frederick. 'We could put things on it.'

To be honest, he wasn't at all sure that this characterless North Kensington sitting-room, devoid of sun at all times, was worthy of his handsome sideboard. But that was not the point. The sideboard's real function, as always, would be to act as a kind of inanimate outrider testing what might lie ahead. If it and Frederick, alike, seemed unhappy in their surroundings, then it and Frederick could leave together. The exit of one, it followed, made the exit of the other so much easier.

'But wouldn't you miss it in *your* room, Freddie?' Lizzie was asking, feeble with consideration. 'I mean, you're so used to it there.'

'It's a sideboard that comes and goes, actually,' answered Frederick mysteriously. 'Besides, I shan't miss it much if I'm here . . . ahem, a little more often, shall I?'

A little more often being but a small step, surely, from *for ever*. Lizzie's joy overflowed.

'Oh, Freddie,' she cried, already seeing in her mind's eye the new *tone* the sideboard would bring to her room – quite apart from the happy relief more of his own presence would bring to her. 'Have it delivered next week. I can hardly believe it.'

'Tomorrow,' said Frederick, thereby inadvertently winding her pleasure to further heights by his impatience. 'It will be your responsibility to furnish it with spirits . . .'

'Of course, of course, dear Freddie.' Quite faint with the prospect of so much good fortune, Lizzie dabbed her eyes with a grubby paper handkerchief pulled from a grubby sleeve, and finished her sherry with more of a swig than a sip.

The sideboard was delivered – a fine piece of Victorian

118

mahogany of elaborate design, with carved flanks and wide drawers that smiled across its highly polished façade. In the small room of utility furniture it stood like an ambassador surrounded by common folk of his kingdom – benign, and yet superior. The gleam of its wood outshone the reckless colour of Lizzie's carpet, its unquestionable solidity emphasised the inferiority of her mean chairs and table of simulated oak.

'Doesn't look at all bad, there,' said Freddie, lying with conviction.

Some days after the arrival of the sideboard he turned up with a trunk of clothes.

'No point in having empty drawers,' he explained, and set about filling them with piles of silk shirts, socks and under-wear. Lizzie's delight, at such manifestation of his intentions, once again bubbled. Already she had invested in several bottles of drink (albeit *half*-bottles). Now, further to show her apprecia-tion, she made no comment when Frederick parked in his usual arrogant fashion on a double yellow line. But despite these measures of compromise – improvements, he grudgingly supposed they were – once Frederick was installed almost permanently in Lizzie's flat (allowing himself just two nights a week at home) he could not deny that all was not well within him.

It was not that Lizzie failed to be appreciative. Of both him and his sideboard (which he had reason to believe she secretly polished every day when he was out) she expressed constant, wearying appreciation. But repetitive praise is no substitute for intellectual stimulation or even, from time to time, a small carnal thrill, if that is what a man is after. And Frederick could not help noticing – for all his attempts to ignore such matters – that since the arrival of the sideboard Lizzie's desire for fun had waned. Perhaps its presence personified to her a gesture of commitment which meant that in certain areas she could now relax: no longer did she nightly offer her demure body in its pink flannelette nightgown. Several times a week the deep sleep of a contented woman overtook her even before he had time to join her in the bed.

But it was just such defects, that could well develop into serious disadvantages should a state of marital relations be negotiated, that the outrider sideboard was employed to detect.

'It's time to move on,' thought Frederick to himself one evening, patting his piece of furniture, not long after the dramatic installation. 'I believe neither of us would be happy in any surroundings designed by Lizzie, ever. But it was only fair to try.'

It occurred to him, as he sat waiting for Lizzie to finish preparing for their evening's adventure at the Odeon, that with the increasing costs of removal men these days his method of future life-testing was a little extravagant. But then Frederick had always prided himself on his skills in matters of diplomacy, and a system that was to work well would naturally be expensive. Comfort lay in the fact that plainly his system *did* work, for he and his sideboard had left with their reputations unharmed many times. Each exit had brought its disappointments, but had failed to impair Frederick's hopes that one day the perfect placing of sideboard and self would be found.

Fired, as always, to act quickly once a decision had come upon him, Frederick braved Lizzie's bewilderment and announced he was no longer tempted by an evening at the Odeon. To temper this blow he hurried out and bought a half-bottle of champagne – no point in making the girl feel uncomfortable with a whole bottle. This he opened with the elaborate flourishes of a man struggling with a jereboam, and filled two miniature sherry glasses before breaking the news.

'Well, Lizzie, I've been thinking. It was a mistake bringing the sideboard here, don't you think? A bit out of place what? I had my doubts all along, you know . . .'

With incredulous eyes Lizzie gazed at him, never for one moment guessing that his feelings about his sideboard were precisely akin to his feelings about herself.

'Perhaps you're right,' she said, not wishing to argue with a man who brought her champagne – besides which she was a girl of obligingly malleable opinions.

'And so I think I shall take it back.'

'Oh, Freddie. Well, of course. Though I shall miss it.'

'One doesn't miss *furniture*,' he said, so scathing of such a sentiment that Lizzie dared reveal nothing further of the dismay in her heart.

The process was reversed. First the shirts left in the trunk, then the empty sideboard. After that Frederick allowed Lizzie a few days of his company during which time he was forced to comment on the lack of furniture in her room, and Lizzie was bound to agree. They reverted to their old pattern of arguing about parking near the cinema. Other things, however, were not as before. Perhaps under the illusion that it was only his sideboard that had left her, Lizzie saw no reason to tempt Frederick further with the nightly contortions that had previously caused her so much effort.

Then one day Frederick said, 'Think I shall have to be off, Lizzie. Be at home more. A man can't be parted from his things, really, can he?'

He left Lizzie for good that very evening. All that remained in his memory was a tray of half-drunk half-bottles, now top-heavily placed on Lizzie's inadequate little table. She mourned him for a while in her own quiet way, but, being of a reasonable disposition, after several nights of uninterrupted sleep, she was able to see her departed lover's point of view. Indeed, she was grateful to him: for a man to leave on his own would mean rejection that might be unbearable. But a man who left to accompany his sideboard showed loyalty, perception, and a rare sense of priority – qualities a girl could only admire.

Moment of Fame

*H*elen Judson guarded to herself only one secret: the route of her afternoon walks. Depending on the weather, and her mood, they were either up through the busy streets of the town to the remains of the battlements, or along the canal towpath. The pleasure of deciding each day which walk she should take was one she kept stubbornly to herself. No matter how much her mother questioned her, on her return, she would only reveal she had been 'around', or 'here and there'. Nothing more.

Only on fine Saturdays were the walks of quite a different kind, and no joy at all. Then, Helen was obliged to wheel her mother along the High Street. The irascible old lady would peer into each shop window and with a squawk of triumph find some new cause for indignation: the price of coffee or shoes, the vulgarity of summer hats. 'But I suppose you've seen all this several times a week, it doesn't surprise you,' Mrs Judson would say, considering her manner of probing to be a subtle one. Helen's response was always of such vagueness as to infuriate Mrs Judson further: still she could not discover where, precisely, Helen had taken her weekday walks, and her daughter's closed face and impenetrable secrecy on this one subject filled Mrs Judson with inexhaustible rage. Determined to invade this only remaining area of her daughter's privacy, she planned one day to abandon her tactic of subtle probing and come right out with it. Ask Helen, straight, what she was up to in her hour of freedom five afternoons each week.

Helen was up to nothing more than seeking relief from the tedium of the house. All she desired was a measure of silence after the perpetual nag of her mother's voice: fresh air after the smell of years of stewed prunes and disinfectant and lily-of-the-valley talcum powder which had permeated every room. Her hour alone each day was a thing to be anticipated all morning, to be recalled during the long, dreary evenings. Neither storms nor snow nor uncomfortable heat would be reason enough to forego its pleasures. In the last fifteen years Helen had only missed three walks, due to some major crisis in her mother's health, which were clearly distinguishable from the very frequent ones of a minor kind.

On a Wednesday in October Helen prepared herself, as usual, for her escape. She settled her mother in the armchair by the window which looked on to a small, perished garden. She plumped up cushions, refilled water glass, straightened shawl, placed the *Radio Times* and bag of knitting within reach. Then she lifted Spot the terrier on to Mrs Judson's chest so that the servile little dog could give its customary lick to the mush of purple cheek and neck. She replaced the dog with some distaste on the floor.

'You going out, dear?' Mrs Judson's assumed surprise never dimmed.

'Just for a while.'

'Don't be long. I've this numbness in my leg. I might be heading for something.'

Helen was never long. A precise hour, neither more nor less. Always warned by some new ailment of her mother that to overstay her hour would be fatal.

She could see it was a sharp, gusty afternoon. Helen plucked from a peg in the dim hallway a mauve scarf into which her mother had crocheted many grumbles for last Christmas. She tucked it into the collar of her gaberdine mac and tightened the laces of her walking shoes. Spot panted eagerly at her feet. Afternoon walks were the highlight of his day, too: though no doubt he felt as little joy in Helen's surly company as she did in his irritating excitement at every familiar corner.

Opening the front door, Helen stood for a moment to feel the dry wind on her face. Spot immediately spurted out into the wizened front garden, yelped in idiot frenzy at the foot of the one remaining standard rose tree whose salmon-pink blooms Helen disliked every June.

'Shut up, you scabby fawning little bitch,' she said out loud, releasing the venom of the morning on the dog, 'or I'll kick your guts in.'

As if ashamed by the violence of the language it had spewed

forth, Helen's pale worm of a mouth concentrated into a single pencil line, lips indistinguishable from skin. She tossed her head – so many grey hairs, now, among the auburn – and made for the canal.

The water, today, lustreless as the sky, was made flaccid by the wind. It trembled like geriatric flesh. Autumnal reminders of death were a comfort to Helen: her mother could not survive many more years, then she would be free to die in peace herself. Such a thought released the warmth of contentment through Helen's meagre body. The minuscule speck of sand she represented in eternity was, at least, a polished one: dutiful life untroubled by ambition or surprise or adventure, to be ended by death that would not cause a single person in the world a moment of regret. Ah! she was fortunate, really. Those well-meaning neighbours who advised she should get out more, sacrifice less to her mother, were foolish in their ignorance. Perhaps they did not understand the pleasure of repaying debts – the childhood years when her mother had been constant in her affection, her puddings and her darning, could not be discounted merely because an accident had turned a well-meaning woman into a selfish, bitter old lady. Besides, there was much to be said for narrowness of life. Helen had no desire to widen her horizons. The rigid cage of her days, for all its petty irritations, was safe. Release, when it came, would be alarming.

Helen was alone, as usual, on the towpath. Few people chose to walk along the muddy banks of the canal, spurned by all wild flowers, though thick with willow herb in August and blackberries in September. Often, the water itself smelt dead. Swallows, dipping low for a glance at their reflections, hastily swooped up again into sweeter air. But the trees were handsome: chestnuts, poplar, ash – their leaves beginning to turn. Cold, suddenly, Helen quickened her step. Some way ahead of her Spot was barking at something beneath the bridge. He was always barking. Years ago Helen had grown immune to the urgency of the sound. She felt no responsibility for him on walks, gave him no instructions. If he cared to follow at heel, she made no comment. If he darted about in his irresponsible fashion she would not concern herself. By all rights he should

127

have been run over long ago. Helen was not going to lessen his chances by giving him advice.

So now she ignored his barking but hurried against the cold. As she approached the bridge, Spot turned to her with his stupid grin, yapping all the while. Then he scampered off to a place on the canal bank a hundred yards farther on.

It was there Helen saw an arm sticking out of the water, then a head. They disappeared. Sluggish ripples covered the place they had been. Helen ran.

When she reached the place on the bank where Spot stood barking, the head emerged again. It was a boy of nine or ten, screaming, muddy, apparently unable to move. Helen whipped off her scarf and threw it towards him. The boy's hand flailed towards it, but missed. He screamed more loudly. Helen flung off her mackintosh and jumped into the water.

Looking back on the events of the afternoon, Helen could never understand why, later, she was to be called a heroine. Certainly she had had no time for heroic thoughts of saving life: it had all happened too quickly for thought of any kind. Acting on instinct, Helen had jumped, and with comparative ease pulled the boy from the water. The hardest part had been climbing back up the steep and slippery bank, aggravated by the boy's wailing and Spot's triumphant barking. Once on land, it took some moments to persuade the boy to give Helen his name and address. He lived not far away. Hand in hand, they hurried to his house.

Sam's mother scolded him for going to forbidden territory – 'I always told you one day you'd fall in, fooling about with sticks like that' – but there was relief in her scolding. She repeated her gratitude to Helen, gave her tea and offered to dry her clothes. But now that the boy was safe Helen's only worry was that she should get home within her allotted hour. To be late would mean abundant questioning, and Helen was determined her mother should know nothing of the small drama.

Mrs Judson, Helen found to her relief, had fallen asleep. This enabled her to change her clothes undetected. As she often did this, after a bath in the afternoon, Mrs Judson did not think anything was amiss. That evening, sitting by the small fire of smokeless fuel while her mother grumbled at the television, Helen went over the events of the afternoon in her mind. She recalled the stab of fear that had made her heart race as it had not done for years: the icy grasp of the water, the vile smell of the mud, the piteous face of Sam and the struggle up the bank. The pictures seemed small and far away. She saw herself acting in them, a detached figure, as in a film. It was only the combined memories of cold, fear and smell that convinced her the rescue had actually happened. By the next morning, the matter was almost erased from her mind.

Two days later she found a small bunch of peonies left on the front doorstep. The attached note said: *With many thanks and love from Sam.* Unnerved, Helen put them in a jar in her room, a place Mrs Judson never entered. Later that day came a further shock. On return from her walk to the battlements Helen found her mother in animated conversation with a strange young man in the sitting-room.

'We've a visitor, Helen,' she crowed. 'How about that? This is Mr John Smith from the *Chronicle*. And he's told me all about what you did the other day *down by the canal.*'

That part of the information was definitely the most interesting to Mrs Judson. Her triumph was total. The pains of the morning were forgotten, her smiles uncontainable.

Helen shook hands with the reporter and sat down, weakly. She saw that he and her mother were drinking tea from the best china cups, and the best tea cosy, slotted with ribbons, warmed the pot. They ate biscuits from a plate of Assorted Cream Centres, normally kept for Sundays or Christmas. Mrs Judson had not been up to such preparations for months, her daughter reflected. But she kept her silence.

'Yes, well,' said Mr Smith. 'Young Sam's mother put me on to you. And a very brave act it was, too, if I may say so.'

'Down by the canal,' added Mrs Judson.

'We on the *Chronicle* would like to do a little story about you, Miss Judson, if you wouldn't mind.' Mr Smith licked his pencil with a biscuit-covered tongue.

'I would mind very much indeed,' said Helen. 'There's no story. I only did what anyone would have done in my place. It was neither dangerous nor very dramatic.'

'Kept it from her mother, all right,' said Mrs Judson.

'Quite the silent heroine,' Mr Smith smiled, thinking of the byline under the headline.

'Never tells me where she goes for her walks, do you, Helen?'

'Furthest *I've* ever gone was rescuing a puppy from a duck pond,' admitted Mr Smith, thinking he would ease Helen's path by confessing his own experience of heroism. He told the story at some length, leaving Helen to observe the curious way his presence affected the room. It was four o'clock, but the normal peace of that time was shattered by the intrusion of this unwanted stranger. Spot lay unusually still on the mat, the dark wallpaper glowered with a strange menace.

'So just a little human story for the *Chronicle*, I'd like,' Mr Smith was saying, having been congratulated by Mrs Judson on his courage in the matter of the puppy. 'You wouldn't mind answering just a few questions, now, would you?'

'My husband, Helen's father, and I made the pages of the *Chronicle* on our wedding day, and then again on our silver anniversary,' interjected Mrs Judson, who had not enjoyed an afternoon so much for years. 'Of course, Helen will tell us whatever we want to know. People will like to read a story like that, won't they, Helen?'

Helen answered the reporter's unanimated questions as shortly and simply as she was able. Her theory that the story was of little interest did not convince Mr Smith: there was no doubt, he assured her, fame would be upon her now.

It was quite dark by the time he left. For this reason, as Helen accompanied him unhappily to the gate, she did not observe another of the *Chronicle's* lively employees hiding behind a hedge: a sudden flash exploded in her face. Momentarily blinded, she stumbled back to the house, slammed the door on Mr Smith's apologies. He had not thought the photographer would cause her such fright.

'So it's *down by the canal* you go,' cooed Mrs Judson, ignoring Helen's distress and still eating biscuits. 'Knew I'd find out one day. There's not much you can keep from your mother.'

* * *

130

The following week a large picture of Helen, startled and open-mouthed, was printed on the front page of the *Chronicle*, beside a smaller one of Sam. The story was headed 'The Silent Heroine by John Smith', who delivered his readers the full range of his journalistic talents in his descriptions of the horror of jumping into a lethal canal to rescue a boy on the point of drowning. His colourful exaggeration caused Helen almost to cry out loud, but she knew any remonstrance would be fuel to her mother's opinions, which already had been wearingly repeated over the last two days. The part of the story that held the keenest delight for Mrs Judson were Mr Smith's closing lines. 'And Miss Judson,' he wrote, 'breathed not a word of her great heroism to anyone. She did not even tell her mother.'

'There,' said Mrs Judson, 'see that? What did I tell you? I'm not the only one who thinks your secrecy is peculiar. It agrees with me in the paper.'

That afternoon, walking up through the High Street to the battlements again (she had not so far returned to the towpath) Helen was smiled at by several strangers. In two shops she was congratulated on her courage, and at a pedestrian crossing a child who said he was Sam's friend shook her by the hand. She arrived home trembling to find four admiring letters from people she did not know, and for several days her walks were interrupted by nods and smiles and words of praise. Haunted by such recognition, Helen decided it was time to return to the towpath. At least, there, she would be alone.

But down by the canal her hopes of a peaceful walk were ended by the presence of a distant figure walking towards her. Helen could see, as he bounced under the bridge, hands in pockets, it was the Reverend Arnold Ludgate, vicar of the parish, a man who in the past had made many a visit to the Judsons to urge them to seek the light of his church, but who had eventually been forced to realise they would never become part of his flock. Spot barked eagerly, alerting the vicar. He looked up, recognising Helen at once, and waved cheerily. It was too late for Helen to turn in the opposite direction. She set her face into an expression of intense preoccupation, hoping it would discourage the vicar from too long a conversation. They approached each other in very different spirits.

A yard or so from the exact spot where the rescue had taken

place they met, and stopped. The Reverend Arnold Ludgate was a man of considerable bounce: his enthusiasm, the balls of his feet and his Adam's apple all bounced in constant unison. Now, at rest physically, an almost visible bounce of spirit danced within him. He smiled his very distinct smile: God had chosen teeth for the vicar that should be his particular cross, and the vicar bore them well, smiling more in a single day than most people manage in a week.

'Ah! Miss Judson.' Smile, smile. Helen noticed his sandy hair was turning grey. 'It must be the good Lord's will we should meet like this. It was my intention to call upon you this evening and offer my humble congratulations. That was a most brave and courageous act you committed, and we in the parish are proud – '

'Thank you,' said Helen. 'But it was nothing. It's been exaggerated out of all proportion.'

'Just hereabouts, was it?' The vicar bounced his small hand in the general direction of the canal.

'Just about here,' Helen agreed. Scanning the offending patch of water, the Reverend Arnold remained for a few moments in silent contemplation.

'Very tricky place,' he said at last. 'Thank God you were here. He certainly moves in mysterious ways.'

'Yes,' said Helen.

'His wonders to perform,' added the vicar.

They stood looking at each other, the wind blowing their rather similiar auburn and grey hair. Helen hoped God might now perform the wonder of releasing her from this unwanted encounter: but He did not oblige.

'As a matter of fact, Miss Judson, I had it in mind to make you a little suggestion. There's to be a most interesting talk at the vicarage on Tuesday the fifth: one of our missionaries back from India. I was wondering if you would care to come along? I think I can guarantee quite a little gathering.' The vicar was all smiles again. He looked at Helen with such suffering expectancy of an acceptance that she judged it easier to agree than to go through the dreary mechanics of being persuaded.

Since her old schoolfriend Jenny had died of cancer five years ago she had not been out for an evening: such invitations that came her way she had refused with such constancy that

132

they were now rare. And anyhow, the fuss of arranging a companion for her mother was too much to contemplate. The idea of a talk at the vicarage was the last thing to tempt her to break her pattern: but the fact was the canal episode had shifted normality in a most disagreeable fashion, leaving her ungrounded, shaken, curiously lost. It was for this reason, perhaps, her normal, strong resolve to decline all invitations was weakened. Unwillingly, she accepted.

'Good, good, *good*,' trilled the vicar, bouncing a little on the path. 'I shall take the liberty of dropping by with some reading matter about the whole subject before then: and in the meantime I shall look forward with immense pleasure, quite immense pleasure, to your joining us.'

Helen nodded briefly, looking at her watch with undisguised impatience. The idea of anyone anticipating pleasure in her company was a responsibility she did not care for, but she knew she stood a poor chance of quelling his enthusiasm.

'I must be off,' she said, grateful for the first time in her life to Spot's impatient barking. 'The dog needs his run.'

The Reverend Arnold arrived with his first lot of reading matter that evening, much to the delight of Mrs Judson who, although not a woman of religious inclination herself, regarded any vicar as a high-class visitor. Small glasses of clouded sherry were produced, and the pattern of a normal evening shattered.

Perhaps the vicar judged his welcome at the Judsons to be a warm one, for he ventured to repeat the visit, armed with more missionary reading matter, some days later. He then took the liberty of dropping round most evenings, with some impeccable excuse, and the bottle of sherry, untouched for years, was soon finished.

On the occasions of his visitations Helen sat quietly listening to the conversation between her mother and the Reverend Arnold, resenting every moment of the old, lost tranquillity. The intrusion of this visitor continued to play havoc with the room as she knew it: the horrible magic of change unnerved her very soul.

It had quite the opposite effect upon Mrs Judson to whom, in her mind's eye, the vicar was already a son-in-law. She refrained from putting this idea to Helen in too crude a fashion, but could not contain a small hint of the ambitions in her heart.

'*If* Arnold's courting, Helen, and I don't say he is, then we ought to get in some more Assorted Creams.'

She was curiously enthusiastic at the thought of Helen's night out at the vicarage, even volunteering to spend the evening on her own, provided Helen was in by eleven. This was a promise Helen was able to make with great ease. She left her mother, settled in rugs for an evening of television, with a lack of enthusiasm that seemed to slow her limbs, making the walk to the vicarage a long one.

The Reverend Arnold was an eager host, and had obviously taken great trouble with preparations for the evening. Twelve assorted chairs were placed in rows in his large, cold sitting-room – into which a collection of feeble electric fires had been scattered: there was sherry, tea and assorted cream biscuits on a table ('inspired by my visits to the Judsons,' he whispered to Helen) and the screen for the slides was set up at the end of the room. After a long wait scarcely filled with small, awkward talk, it seemed that only five others besides Helen had decided to give up their evening to the missionary's talk. The spare chairs were left, however, to give the illusion of a larger audience, and in the darkened room, punching away at the slides, the gallant missionary disguised any disappointment he may have felt at the lack of audience, booming his message across as if addressing a packed Albert Hall.

The lecture over, the pale lamps lit again, the vicar's guests now at least had something positive to talk about over their biscuits and tea. But the discussion petered out quickly as a chill wind rattled through the windows, making the thin curtains shudder, and the small patches of warmth from the fires evaporated in the cold air. They made their excuses, the guests, and left. Even the missionary had to be on his way. Helen's inclination was to leave with the others, but something in the vicar's face, behind his bouncing smile, touched her conscience. So when he suggested she might like a nightcap in his study before the journey home, she agreed.

The study, it was true, was warm: a small brown room, bookshelves to the ceiling, a disorganised desk, two armchairs whose life seemed almost spent.

'Only real warm spot in the house,' said the vicar. 'I more or less live in this room.' He poured two minute glasses of thick dark sherry, gave one to Helen, and took the chair opposite her. 'Trouble is, this is a vast house, falling to pieces, and much too big for one man. They're considering pulling it down and building a nice modern box instead, but I don't know when that will be. So meantime I rattle around.' He smiled, uncomplainingly. 'Would that I had a relation to accommodate in one wing – it could be very nice with a lick of paint and a few gas fires. But sadly my dear mother departed from this world in 1947, so there's no one . . .'

'No,' said Helen.

They listened to the wind.

Helen sipped the horrible sweet sherry. She did not want to be sitting here in the vicar's study wearing her polite face. Were she at home she would be in the silent privacy of her own room by now, shawl about her shoulders, *Persuasion* in her hand, the clamps of dull routine an inestimable pleasure. Until the time came that her mother died, and dreaded freedom was thrust upon her, she wanted no change.

The Reverend Arnold had dragged a duster from the skirts of his armchair and was polishing the toe of an already shining shoe with some fervour. His head cast down, Helen was unable to observe his expression as he spoke.

'My dear Miss Judson – may I take the liberty of saying this? I hope I have not alarmed you by my attentions since your great act of heroism. But perhaps it will come as no great surprise to you when I admit it was not *merely* to deliver papers pertaining to our missionary's work that I called upon you quite so frequently . . .'

Rub, rub, rub at the shoe. 'I have grown to feel we are kindred spirits, you and me. Lonely souls, despite the love of our Father.' He ceased polishing at last, returned the duster to its hiding place, and with great effort met Helen's eye. 'You understand? This huge house, ridiculous for one: the Granny wing – dear *Mrs* Judson, I could not but help thinking . . .' He blushed, fervent, but without bounce. 'I mean, there is work to be done, children to be raised, partners to be chosen. I cannot help thinking that God in his mercy has guided me . . .'

Helen stood up, face impassive. The vicar leapt up too, wringing his small hands.

'Forgive me, dear Helen, if I've intruded into areas – '

'I must go,' said Helen. 'I promised Mother I'd be home by eleven.'

The vicar followed her through cold dark passages to the front door.

'Perhaps, at least, you would not reject my suggestion as totally out of hand.' Helen pulled on her gloves. The vicar winced at her small, impatient frown. 'Perhaps you would think it over? I don't want to rush anything: you must forgive me if I've been too hasty – I'm not a man practised at courting.' He managed the faintest smile. 'But unless you give me firm orders not to, I shall take the opportunity of visiting you further, see how things go from there . . .'

Helen looked at him. He shivered in the doorway, Adam's apple bouncing up and down on the dog's collar in silent fear.

'Mr Ludgate,' she said, voice so tight she feared he might hear the cracks, 'thank you for a very pleasant evening. If you'd like to drop round, sometimes, I'm sure my mother and I would be very pleased to see you. But please, I ask you this: don't speak to me again of such things as you have mentioned tonight. You may find it hard to understand, but it's not in my nature to want change. My mother and I are happy as we are.'

'I shall be there,' said the vicar, hope rising like mercury through his body and causing him a familiar bounce of joyous expectation, 'and we shall see what the Good Lord has in store for us.'

They shook hands. Helen, scarf pulled tight round her neck, set off on the walk home, down by the canal where a full moon floated on the still, black water, where the huge trees crackled in the wind. Above the roofs of the town the dark sky was pink as a sore, its edges puffed with cloud. Ruined evenings, blasted life, bitter cold: Helen walked fast, not thinking.

Such Visitors

Miranda Wharton did not agree with the widely held opinion that it is a foolish thing for those in the same profession to marry. She had heard all the pessimistic theories many times: the endless shop talk, the narrowness of vision, the rivalry, and believed them to be nonsense. Indeed, she and her husband Jim, who had been married for seventeen happy years, were proof of their inaccuracy.

Miranda and Jim were both teachers of English, though it has to be said that their special periods were divided by a century. For a couple of years they had even taught in the same university, with no ill effects. They rarely discussed their work at home – not a conscious decision, this; it was just that Jim seemed keener to talk about canoeing (a long-time hobby) and Miranda was too busy with running the house, experimenting with Italian cookery, and being a conscientious mother to their fifteen-year-old daughter, Sally.

As far as they could tell, there was no rivalry between them either. Friends sometimes put this – the most obvious of the assumed disadvantages – to them. How had Miranda felt, they asked, when Jim was made a senior lecturer? Delighted, Miranda had replied laughingly, and meant it. She herself, at present Writer in Residence at a college in Southampton, was much in demand to lecture all over the country on the Romantic poets and, her real love, Thomas Hardy. Her many published papers had received acclaim in academic circles: she enjoyed the writing, she enjoyed the lecturing – in a word, she was more than happy in her work. Jim was equally satisfied with his post in the university, though continually incredulous at the shockingly low standard of literacy among his pupils. 'They can't construct a simple sentence, let alone an essay,' he sometimes grumbled to Miranda, and often contemplated the return to being a school teacher so that he could try to inculcate the *basic principles* of English into their heads at an early age. He vaguely kept an ear open for some suitable post at a school, but so far nothing had come up. So life for the Whartons continued on its contended way, their good fortune appreciated by both. That was a subject often discussed: not smugly, heaven forbid, but with gratitude to God for their blessed lot. (They were both practising Christians, though had to travel fifteen miles every Sunday, now, to find a church with a 1662 service. Not for them the bastardised language, and all that embarrassing hand-shaking, of the misguided New Way to attract worshippers.) In a word, and without wishing to seem complacent, Miranda Wharton often thought that she and Jim must be one of the luckiest married couples of their acquaintance.

One Tuesday morning in mid-May, Miranda sat alone in a first-class compartment of an inter-city train bound for Bristol. She was to speak at a college of adult education about The Dark in Hardy's Poems, a talk she had given on several occasions and which had gone down very well. To be honest, she would have preferred to talk about the *light* in his poems: that would have taxed her harder, meant something to struggle with. But The Dark had been especially requested, so the only challenge would be to make it sound as fresh and vibrant as the first time she had given it.

But for the moment she was thinking neither about the dark nor the light in Hardy, but about the wisdom of Tom Stoppard. The night before, the Whartons had gone to London to see *The Real Thing* – a trip to the theatre, with a modest dinner afterwards, was a treat they afforded themselves once a month. They were both much impressed by the play, decided to see it a second time. Jim loved the famous cricket bat speech – marvellous stuff, he declared: Stoppard was wizard at enlightening the ordinary. Who else had ever before pointed out that a cricket bat is sprung like a dance hall? '*"What we're trying to do is to write cricket bats"*,' he quoted, chuckling, on the way home.

Miranda, although she did not mention it to Jim, was more taken by another speech. She had tried to remember it, but was annoyed to find, later that night, she could only recall a few words – something about politeness. Henry's explanation to Annie about not wanting anyone else had given Miranda what she called her entry-into-a-cathedral feeling: goose pimples, and a tingling down the spine. And then, this morning, she had left the house extra early so as to have time to stop in at the bookshop on the way to the station. Jim hadn't noticed her premature start, but all the same she felt curiously guilty, as if she harboured a secret whose nature she did not quite understand.

She had bought a copy of the play, finished it by Reading. After that she tipped her head back, letting her eyes glide over the rapid fields emerald with early May, lilac trees buxom in cottage gardens, clumps of flame-yellow broom. She had found the passage, read it several times. It had made her cold again – physically, excitingly cold. She picked it up again – for the last time, she told herself. The words, by now, she had almost by heart:

'*I'm your chap . . . I don't want anyone else but sometimes, surprisingly, there's someone, not the prettiest or the most available, but you know that in another life it would be her. Or him, don't you find? A small quickening. The room responds lightly to being entered. Like a raised blind. Nothing intended, and a long way from doing anything, but you catch the glint of being someone else's possibility, and it's a sort of politeness to show you haven't missed it . . .*'

'Someone else's possibility,' Miranda repeated to herself. Her heart was beating against the hum of the train. She had never experienced any such thing, but she thought she could imagine it.

Shortly before arriving in Bristol, Miranda found herself indulging in a moment of rare self-assessment. She looked down at her skirt, her jersey: the one, khaki twill, the other white cotton. She had never dressed in order to be anything but comfortable – the world of fashion was a remote one in which she had no interest or aspirations. But this sudden, critical look at herself brought a twinge of dissatisfaction. How, today, in her workmanlike beige and white, would she strike a stranger, a *possibility*, striding down the train? Not very forcibly, she thought.

To double check, she looked at herself in the small mirror of

141

her powder compact. The slight, scornful smile caused a surprising amount of wrinkles at the corners of her pale mouth. She moved on up to the eyes, preparing herself for further disappointment. Jim had once told her that it was the mischief of her pretty eyes that had first drawn him to her. Where had all the mischief gone in middle age, she wondered? And were they still pretty? Striving for honesty, it was hard to say. She snapped shut the compact, ran her hand through her thick, bouncing hair which seemed to lead a turbulent life of its own. She wondered if the habitually vain were ever immune to the truth.

Miranda sat on the narrow bed in the sliver of a room that had been assigned to her with little ceremony. Its walls were whitewashed breeze block. The light was a single central bulb with a raffia shade shaped like a coolie. As always, Miranda wondered who could be behind such design. What was he like, the architect who woke up one morning and decreed that whitewashed breeze block and a ceiling light would be agree-able for students and visiting lecturers? She was familiar with such places, having stayed in them all over the country – jerry-built buildings, circa 1960, with their miles of sour neon lighting, and cheerless lecture halls where chairs screamed on synthetic floors. But she had never managed to become imper-vious to their ugliness.

She flipped through the typewritten agenda. The conference was to last three days, although her own visit was to be brief. Her lecture was at eight p.m., after supper: she would return home on an early train tomorrow. She observed that many subjects, popular at such gatherings, were to be lectured upon by a dozen experts she had never heard of. And then, curiously, she saw the name of Ivan Whiteham-Jones, described in the programme as the definitive writer on Eliza-bethan literature. What on earth . . .? It seemed, even more peculiar, he was to give a talk on Messages in the Modern Novel and How to Detect Them. *Quite* outside his own subject. Perhaps, thought Miranda, Mr W-J found, like her, the need for money meant that the quality of an audience could not always be a consideration.

Ivan Whiteham-Jones was engaged to speak today, at four p.m. *Now*, in fact, Miranda realised, looking at her watch. Even now the eminent man was in some lecture hall enchanting an audience of aspiring writers. Miranda had watched him with admiration on many occasions on the television, and had read every one of his books. But she had never had the opportunity to hear him lecture. That chance had now gone. It was time for tea. Annoyed with herself, Miranda left the room.

In the canteen, she found rain slashing against the vast plate-glass windows with all the viciousness of storm waves against a pier. Miranda sat alone at a table, drinking tea from a plastic beaker. All round her, dozens of mature students enthused about Ivan Whiteham-Jones. His lecture had been a great success, it seemed.

'I was so carried away I never took a note,' confessed a nearby grey-haired woman. She patted at her crocheted jersey as if to calm the excitement of her skin that the lecture had caused her. Lucky Mr W-J, Miranda thought. He could now go home.

She saw him at the end of a long queue, waiting for tea at the canteen, and the vast room responded lightly. Back to her, she could see his concentration on a tray of doughnuts was interrupted several times by congratulations. In acknowledgement, he nodded politely, untouched by the appreciation. Miranda found herself critical of the cut of his trousers, the dreadful diamond pattern of his lambswool jersey, the rubber soles of his clumsy shoes. Other people's clothes usually made little impact on her. Why was she so perturbed by Ivan Whiteham-Jones's lack of sartorial instinct? And another question: why, like her, had he chosen to ignore the special room for lecturers, and come to the canteen?

Ivan Whiteham-Jones turned, eyes upon his tray of tea. Miranda could now quite clearly see his face, familiar from television – dark eyes, hair falling over his forehead, extraordinarily beautiful mouth. A small quickening, she felt, and stirred her tea. Her eyes followed him to a far corner of the room. He sat at an unoccupied table, drank gloomily, studied the agenda. His air of preoccupation was plainly designed to deter students from eagerly seeking further advice.

At six-thirty in the large hall, Miranda found that she and

143

Whiteham-Jones were placed next to each other at a long table on the platform, both part of a panel to answer random questions from the students below. Yellow-grey light squeezed through the high, prison-like window. The audience itself was a little blurred, as if seated in mist. Their waves of earnest anticipation rustled between the walls of the ubiquitous breeze block. They scrutinised scraps of paper on which they had composed very long and serious questions.

Ivan Whiteham-Jones shook Miranda's hand. Smiled. Mockingly? It was so quick a smile Miranda could not be sure.

'Glad I've been put next to the star turn,' he said. 'I've always wanted to hear your Hardy. Delighted to meet you.'

There was no time for Miranda to convey her own delight. The chairman was on his feet, clearing his throat, polishing his hands.

'Ladies and gentlemen, *writers all*,' he began, with the professional tact of one bent on raising the fee for next year's conference. Twenty minutes later the questions began.

'Could anyone on the panel be so kind as to tell me if publishers would prefer us to send in our work double-spaced on A4 paper, or would it go against us if we wrote on a small size? You see, I can never get used to an A4. It hinders the *flow*, somehow, I find.'

The questioner had a chestnut rinse and a melon-pink tracksuit. She was plainly a veteran conference-goer, not afraid to get the whole thing off to a good start with an apt question. For a moment she basked in sympathetic murmurs all round her. Then she took up her pencil, poised to record the answer she was about to receive.

Miranda noticed the chairman looking with unconcealed desperation along his panel of experts. It was as if he had hoped the opening question might have started on a higher level . . . though experience had taught him how obsessed with practicalities these mature students could be. Ivan Whiteham-Jones obligingly caught his eye. At the same time, W-J's clenched fist gently bounced on Miranda's hand, signal of some private joke. Having come all this way, I for one am prepared to enter into the spirit of the thing, he seemed to say. In a trice, he was on his feet, and dealt masterfully with the problem of the typing paper most likely to succeed. Having

144

eloquently put the worried lady's mind at rest, he sat down again, turned to Miranda. Her heart was beating ludicrously fast. She met his smile.

The questions finally over, members of the panel were shown into a room of yet more whitewashed breeze block, though here there had been some attempt to enliven the walls with abstract paintings, the work of past students. A long table was laid with sullen salads, hard-boiled eggs humped under lustreless mayonnaise, pallid pink meats faintly mottled and thinly sliced, bowls of tinned fruit: the kind of food not enhanced by overhead lighting. Miranda had no appetite. She found Ivan at her side, holding out a glass of white wine.

'Grab something to eat and let's make for that corner,' he said.

Miranda chose a slice of stale French bread, a minuscule packet of butter in gold paper, and a sliver of cheese.

'I suppose you're off any moment,' she said. 'I'm sorry I missed your lecture.'

'No, I'm here for the night, in fact. Appointment nearby, in the morning. So at least I'll be able to hear yours.' He gave a brief, restless smile. 'You didn't miss anything not coming to mine – not my normal subject, as you can imagine. But I had to be here anyway, so I did it as a favour to Jack.'

He nodded towards the chairman, who, far, far away among the other lecturers, poked at his food, sipped his wine, laughed politely under the vicious white lights.

They sat on low chairs of acrylic tweed, their plates on a lower table between them. Miranda knew she would remember for ever the feeling of the scratchy stuff behind her knees, and the geometric patterns on the plates.

'I was supposed to have rung my wife an hour ago,' Ivan was saying, looking at his watch, 'but I couldn't find a telephone that worked.' There was purpose in his voice.

'Maddening,' said Miranda. She sipped at her wine, ignored the bread and cheese.

'So,' said Ivan, another limited smile uptilting his bewitching mouth, 'here I am, meeting you at last. I've read all your papers, you know. You could say I was quite a fan. But I'd always imagined you . . . well, older, I suppose.'

145

Miranda felt the blood rushing to her face and lowered her head.

'I've read all *your* books, naturally,' she said.

'Have you really?'

He sounded surprised. His eyes were so hard upon her she was forced to raise her own and meet them. She put down her glass with a shaking hand. Her heart was battering audibly. She knew Ivan observed all this.

'Look, my hand's shaking too,' he said, quietly. 'Now isn't that indeed a peculiar thing? How do you explain that? Two people shaking, and they've scarcely met.'

Miranda gave a slight laugh. She tried to compose herself, resist this dangerous ground.

'I'd like to take my chance,' she said, 'to talk to you about Donne. I mean, about anything. But particularly about Donne.' She cursed herself for her own confusion.

'Ah, Donne.' Ivan sighed. 'Well, Donne would call this "our first strange and fatal interview", wouldn't he? Don't deny it, now.' He laughed, lightening the moment. 'Listen, there's so little time. To hell with Donne when there's so little time. Unless that's what you'd really like. *Is* that what you'd really like? Tell me, honestly.'

'No, no,' conceded Miranda, and they both laughed.

What I'd really like, a voice within her said, is to take a speedboat to the moon with this man, talk to him for years, say things I've never said before which would need no words. I'd like to walk on beaches with him, climb hills, sit by fires while he read poems in that dappled voice . . . All that sort of fantastical rubbish. She twisted herself upright with a jerk, reclaimed her glass with a hand that was still shaking.

'Alas, the negotiating of souls needs a little time,' Ivan went on, 'once the light has struck blindingly. There you are, some Donne for you mixed with a pinch of Reid . . .' They both looked up to see the chairman approaching. 'But promise me, afterwards, a drink somewhere?'

Miranda smiled brilliantly at the chairman. She wanted, dottily, to let him know of her irrepressible exhilaration.

'You two known each other long, have you?' he asked.

'For ever and ever, in a way,' said Ivan.

* * *

As she stood on the platform looking down at a blotched mass of faces she could not distinctly see, Miranda felt nervous. Her hands were still shaking. She held them behind her back, and leaned against the bare table to steady herself. Eventually, the shuffling and whispering and the squeaking of chairs ceased, and the silence in the hall was rampant, white-lit, frightening. The Dark in Hardy, Miranda said to herself. Ivan was somewhere at the back. She could not see him, and was glad. The silence continued, but the familiar opening words of the lecture she had given a dozen times had quite disappeared from her mind. Then she heard a distant voice, her own, and was aware that the quality of her audience's listening was almost tangible.

'Why did you give no hint that night,' she began in a low voice,

> That quickly after the morrow's dawn,
> And calmly, as if indifferent quite,
> You would close your term here, up and be gone
> Where I could not follow
> With wing of swallow
> To gain one glimpse of you even anon?
>
> Never to bid goodbye,
> Or lip me the softest call,
> Or utter a wish for a word, while I
> Saw morning harden upon the wall,
> Unmoved, unknowing
> That your great going
> *Had placed that moment, and altered all . . .*

She stopped abruptly.

There had been no time to think. She had begun quoting spontaneously, some instinct telling her to send a private message to Ivan. There was no need to go on.

'That was the beginning of a poem called "The Going",' she said, 'which, I think you will agree . . .' She was off, back in command, no longer shaking, her audience in her hands.

When the applause was over and the listeners all gone, Miranda found Ivan waiting for her by the door.

'We're invited,' he said, 'to join the others for a nightcap

147

back in that sterile room. But we won't be doing that, will we? We're going somewhere else. It won't be the sort of place I'd like to take you, but anything to get out of here.'

They hurried from the relentless white of the college building, down a deserted High Street, into a crowded pub of amber lights and glinting tankards on tartan walls. Miranda scarcely took in the practicalities. Somehow they were at a small, beer-ringed table, with two glasses of whisky.

'That was very, very good,' Ivan said. 'I could have listened all night. You had the old things absolutely enraptured. But I don't want to talk about Hardy, or Donne, or even Shakespeare, if you don't mind.' Against the background thump of taped music it was quite hard to hear his voice. He clenched his fist, thumped the table. Then he placed it on Miranda's hand, and left it there.

'I'm a happily married man, at last,' he said.

'And I've been a happily married woman for seventeen years,' responded Miranda, her voice unwittingly shrill, defensive.

'There we are then, in precisely the same situation. That's good.' He sighed. 'It's funny, though, isn't it? You come to a conference, expecting nothing. I never expect anything. And then the gods play tricks on you. Show you temptation. Upset the equilibrium. Physically shake you. All in – what? A matter of hours. What's it all about? Don't just widen your pretty eyes at me like that – *tell me*.'

'I can't,' said Miranda.

Ivan was standing, restless. Barely ten minutes in the pub, Miranda noted.

'Come on. We must go back. I've a mass of stuff to read before the morning.'

He took her hand and led her through the bright, laughing people to the sharper air of the car park. A discreet moon lit geometrical shapes on the metal of the cars. In the office blocks that jutted up all round them the uniform windows were stuck in flatly silvered rows, sharp as flints.

'Let's pretend we're not here,' said Ivan. He kissed her, kissed her.

When eventually they pulled apart, Miranda knew that nothing had been intended, and they were a long way from doing anything more. Ivan's face was mostly in shadow, but splinters of moonlight flared in his eyes. He spoke quietly, all the brusqueness gone.

'I've always had this thought, you see, that we're all such visitors in each other's lives – mere visitors. Even husbands and wives. Visitations are all we can manage, really: perhaps all we should require.' He paused. 'I know what I'd *like*, of course. Apart from anything else, I'd like to come and find you one day, spend a little innocent time with you. But I don't believe in acting wilfully against the grain, do you?'

'No.'

'Endangering things?'

'No.'

'So this visit, this short, short visit, has to be over. I'm sorry.' He kissed Miranda again, lightly on the forehead this time, and put a hand on her neck. 'There's a dreadful irony, isn't there, in the two faces of recognition?' He gave a small laugh. 'On the one hand, the joy. On the other, such sadness, having to deny . . . But still, the fact is, we've met. At least we've met.'

'We've met, yes,' said Miranda.

In silence they walked back to the college, swung through the plate-glass doors, stood dazed for a moment by the unkind whiteness of the lights. Ivan touched her chin with a teasing finger, smiled.

'Never confuse me with a pure Elizabethan,' he said. 'Hardy's my man, just as much as yours, that's why I've always read you with such interest. And Hardy it was who said – didn't he? – "Goodbye is not worth while".' Then he turned away quickly and was gone, dissolved into the glare of the long white corridor, on his way to some single bedroom identical to Miranda's own.

She sat up, awake, all night, watched the morning harden, allowed herself a few fantasies about Ivan Whiteham-Jones, and then attempted to discard them. She arranged herself to go home, and when she arrived there she was pleased, as always, to be welcomed by her husband and her daughter.

Somehow, she did not mention to Jim that she had met Ivan. They were long past the stage of reporting what had gone on at each other's conferences. Besides, there was nothing of substance that could be told. But in the rhythm of normality that swiftly returned, the glint of possibility she had now experienced flickered its small light in her soul, reminding her in some disturbing way that it had 'altered all'. As she continued in her happy marriage, Miranda found herself hoping, for a while, there might be some word from Ivan, and then she found herself surreptitiously looking out for him. Once she heard him (that voice!) on the radio; another time she caught his last few moments on a television programme. At Christmas, as a sort of politeness, and to show she had not missed whatever had been recognised and denied at the conference, she sent him a card, care of his university. He did not send one back, but then she did not expect he would. None the less, she could not quite forget this brief visitor, this man who, in another life, might have been hers.

The Weighing Up

*T*he last time I weighed myself, yesterday morning to be precise, the scales registered twelve stone and one ounce. That is not a record. I have been several pounds heavier. On rare occasions, these last five years, and quite by chance, I've also been a pound or so lighter.

You may be surprised by my saying this, and possibly not believe me, but I am not depressed by my weight. Passing shop windows, or the occasional glance in a mirror, confirm that all hope of ever retrieving my old, slight shape, has quite gone. And I don't mind.

The funny thing is, nor does Jeremy. We married twenty-three years ago when I was a mere slip of a thing – an old joke was that he referred to me as a *slipover* rather than a pushover. Food, then, did not concern me much. I cooked because I had to: meals for the children, dinner for Jeremy on the rare occasions he was home. But I did make quite an effort, for years, with Sunday lunch. There were constant disputes about whether it should be chocolate pudding or Brown Betty (as a family, we all love apples) each week. I made whatever they finally decided upon, and enjoyed their appreciation.

It was after Sam and Kathy left for university and only Laura, our youngest, was left at home, that I became unstuck. The trouble was, used to making enough for five healthy appetites, I miscalculated when cooking for two. I always made too much, to be on the safe side. There were always things left over. Remembering the post-war economy of my own childhood, and not liking to see things go to waste, I found it hard to leave them in the fridge or larder to await reheating. It became impossible to throw them away. Finishing them off myself – cold rice pudding for elevenses, cold chicken curry for tea, time doesn't matter to an anarchistic eater – became my habit.

By the time Laura finally left, too, to go to Durham, I had noticed the conspicuous change in my figure. I should have taken some strong hold – gone on a diet, changed my eating habits, whatever. But no. One of the pleasures I came to look forward to was a proper three-course dinner alone in front of the television. Plus half a bottle of Jeremy's nice white wine. He always said, 'Help yourself from the cellar whenever you want to,' and I would take him at his word. Another pleasure was breakfast: all those fried glistening things I had cooked for years for the children and never eaten myelf, I now found immensely enjoyable. They gave a good start to the morning. They would keep me going till the chocolate biscuits and coffee at eleven, later followed by homemade bread and soup for lunch.

The children, when they came home, teased me mildly about my middle-aged spread. They found it odd I had put on so much weight considering I seemed to be eating no more than usual. For, out of habit, or perhaps secret shame, in front of them I remained quite abstemious, piling their plates with second and third helpings but toying with just one small helping myself. I contemplated confessing to them my secret vice, but then couldn't face it. Besides, they didn't go on about it, accepted me lovingly as always. As for Jeremy – home less than ever despite retirement being only four years off – he made no comment at all.

Jeremy is in shipping. It has always been his job, ever since he came down from Balliol. I'm ashamed to say after twenty-three years of marriage I still don't know *precisely* what it is he does in shipping. Sales, I think. 'Do you have to sell a liner like a man who sells double glazing?' I once asked, but he was concentrating on something else, or perhaps considered it a question not worth answering, though he would never have been so rude as to say so.

For Jeremy is a very kind man. In matters of consideration, you could not fault him. That is not to say he is a man of declarations. His appreciation is expressed in other ways. Compliments have never sprung readily from his lips, and indeed I'm sometimes unsure he even observes things that might inspire other men to words of praise: Laura's new short hair, or one of my better soufflés, for instance. And yet he plainly cares deeply for his family. When he *is* home – and his business takes him all over the world, sometimes for weeks on end, for most of the year – he gives us his full attention. He asks questions, goes for walks with Sam, talks about Renaissance poets to Kathy and the history of politics to Laura, and takes an interest in my herbaceous border and the state of my old-fashioned roses. 'Sorry I've got to go again,' he says, when his time is up. And I know he means it. He looks full of regret.

Away from us, he sends postcards, calls occasionally at inconvenient hours – though, heavens, the sound of his voice is never inconvenient – from Australia or wherever. I always get a decent warning of his homecoming. Mrs Manns, his secretary, gives a ring saying what time he is due at Heathrow, so there is no chance of my letting him down. A company chauffeur meets him at the airport these days, but I can be sure of having ready his favourite shrimp vol-au-vents, or risotto, or, best of all, baked red mullet. Plus, of course, a bottle of good wine in the fridge.

He always seems to be pleased to be home. Lately, he's taken to bringing me chocolates. He apologises they have come from the airport, time being very scarce – but they're invariably very expensive and elaborately beribboned. Particularly good, of course, when he returns from Brussels or Zurich. We have established a funny little routine after our first reunion dinner: I offer him one of the heavenly chocolates: he refuses. 'You have them all for yourself,' he says with his generous smile. And once he's gone away again – I don't open them till then – that's just what I do.

I'm sitting now by the study fire, the latest box – a fine assortment of soft centres – by my side. I've watched the nine o'clock news, and *Panorama*, and am quite content. I choose my third – fourth? fifth, perhaps? – and last for the evening: a walnut cluster. The hand that plucks it, I notice, is a plump, puffed-up thing compared with what it used to be. The nails are still a pretty shape, but my wedding ring sits deep beside two banks of flesh. I could never get it off, now: it will have to be buried with me. The ankles and feet, stretched out, match the hands in puffiness. No longer can I wear the pretty shoes that I used to love to find, and which caused people to pay many a compliment. The arms are large and heavy. Once delicate wrist and elbow bones now quite obliterated by fat, and the stomach is swollen to the same size as when I was six months pregnant. None of these things worries me dreadfully, but I do observe them. Thank God we are designed so as not to see our own faces – that was an almighty piece of tact on the Lord's part. For on the occasions I'm forced to study the face, I admit to a certain desolation. Simply because it doesn't look like the one I remember best. 'If you'd just lose a stone or two, Mum,' Laura said a week or so ago, 'you'd be exceptionally good-looking. I mean, you've got the features. It's just that they're becoming obscured.'

It's true. (Laura has always been the most loving and most honest of the children. She's the one who minds most about this metamorphosis.) I did have fine eyes: but as the cheeks have swollen their size has diminished. And the once pointed chin is now indeterminate, mingling with underchins that ripple down to a doughy chest. My hair still shines from time to time, I think. But I'm not attractive any more. I'm fat, fat, fat.

Perhaps if Jeremy were to complain, I would make a serious effort to do something about it. This I reflect on sometimes: I am so much less busy now and have time for introspection. (A dangerous pastime, I always think. I don't indulge too often.) But as Jeremy does not complain, and remains as considerate to me and appreciative of home life as he is able in the brief times he is here, why make the effort? As it is, I am peaceful, lazier these days, and happy. And it's time to go to bed.

It's a windy night. Draughts slightly move the curtains. The weather forecast warned of tempestuous autumn days ahead. Well, if it rains tomorrow I shall stay at home with bean soup for lunch, and make a list of ingredients for the Christmas cake. Some people might be daunted by my solitary days of trivial pursuits. I like them. Besides, it's not a barren life. There is always Jeremy's next return to look forward to.

Yesterday he rang from Tokyo to say he doubted if he could get home by the weekend. He would ring again if plans changed. I stir, meaning to get up. The telephone on the table beside me rings. It can only mean that plans *have* changed.

'Hello?' says a woman. I do not know her voice. 'Is that Ada Mullins?'

'Avril,' I say.

'Sorry. I knew it was something beginning with A. Couldn't for the life of me remember what.' She gave a small laugh, but not a friendly one.

'Who are you?' I ask.

'I'm Richenda Gosforth.'

Silence.

'Richenda . . .?'

I do not know a Richenda, I'm almost sure. Perhaps she's a friend of one of the children.

'Gosforth.' Silence for a moment or two. 'I'm the mother of Jeremy's baby. Your husband Jeremy.'

'Yes, yes. I know Jeremy's my husband,' I say. My fingers fiddle with the velvet ribbon twisted into a multi-looped bow on the lid of the chocolate box. I feel very calm.

'Look, Av – Mrs Mullins,' says Richenda Gosforth. 'Jeremy wanted to keep all this from you. He'll probably be livid with me when he finds out I've rung you. But I think you should know the truth.'

'Really?' I say, but is isn't really a question as I'm not sure what she's talking about.

'Well, the truth is, Jeremy and I have been together for nearly two years now. I've been like a second wife to him in a way. I suppose you could say I've had all the glamour but none of the real advantages.'

'None of the real advantages?' I echo.

'Absolutely not. I mean, yes, I've had the trips abroad, the first-class flights, the champagne, the hanging about in hotel suites while he's in his conferences. But what I've never had with Jeremy is a *base*. That's been your privilege. You've got the base with Jeremy.'

'That's true,' I say. 'Jeremy and I have certainly had a solid base for a good many years now. Man and wife.'

'Exactly. And you hold the trump card, *being* his wife.'

'I am his wife, yes.' Another pause.

'You're being very nice,' continues Richenda Gosforth. 'I thought you'd be screaming mad at me. I had to have three whiskys before making this call. Anyhow, about the baby. I thought you should know about the baby. When I first told Jeremy, heavens, was he put out! Wanted to whizz me off to

157

an abortionist straight away. He didn't want anything to *rock the boat*, as he put it.'

'That's always been a concern of his, not to rock the boat,' I reflect. We give a small, clashing laugh. When the laughter dies, Richenda Gosforth goes on with her story.

'But I said: no way, Jeremy. I'm not going to be pushed about for your convenience. My baby's not going to be murdered just to suit you. I'm going to have it.'

'Quite right,' I say, being anti-abortion myself, and to end another silence.

'Jason was born three weeks ago,' says Richenda, 'and when Jeremy saw I had no intention of changing my mind, I must say he was very decent about it all. He set me up in this flat near Richmond Park, and he's paying for a part-time nanny so I'll be able to go back to work. He was in Canada for the actual birth, but he comes to see us as often as he can. I'm expecting him for the weekend when, I've told him, we've finally got to thrash things out.'

'He'll be with *you*, this weekend?' I say. 'To thrash things out?'

'Exactly. Unless, that is, his plans change, and he can't make it.'

I feel the merest smile twitch the corners of my mouth. 'His plans do change,' I say.

'I'm sorry if all this is coming as an awful shock to you,' says Richenda. 'But I thought if I could tell Jeremy I'd spoken to you, although he might be angry, it would make things easier.'

'I hope so,' I said.

It might not make things *much* easier, I think, Jeremy not being a man who thrives on confrontation.

'The thing is *this*. In a word, Mrs Mullins, Jeremy is the love of my life. I want to marry him. I think, to be honest, he feels the same.'

She is silent again. I feel I should help her out.

'And I'm the stumbling block,' I say.

'Exactly. You're the stumbling block. Jeremy's told me a million times he can't leave you, break up the family. *Yet*, anyway. *Some time*, he says, perhaps. But he says he can't bring himself to leave you at the moment, whatever he feels for me and Jason, for reasons he can't explain. You're a taboo subject, actually. So I don't know anything about you. I don't know if you're old or young or middle-aged, fat or thin, whether you work or not, whether you're a good wife and mother. I don't know *anything* about you. Jeremy goes all blank if I ask any questions. He simply won't talk about you – ' She breaks off with a sob in her voice. I wait for her to recover. 'Mrs Mullins, forgive me for saying this, but although he keeps his silence I get the impression that *there's not much going on between you and Jeremy*. Would you mind if he left you?'

I see my dimpled fingers twirl faster through the pretty loops of the velvet bow. Would I mind if he left me? It is a question I have never asked myself.

'It's a question I've never asked myself,' I tell Richenda Gosforth, 'and a question I trust I shall never have the need to ask myself.'

I glance down at my feet, slumped inwards upon themselves, conveying the weariness that seemed to be congealing my veins, making me hungry. I lift the lid from the chocolate box and rustle through the crisp, empty, pleated brown-paper cases that once held the delicious collection of soft centres.

'Oh,' says Richenda Gosforth, eventually. 'Really?'

She does not sound deflated. She's obviously a determined young woman (I presume young, anyway) out to get her own way.

'Well, I think you should think about it all, if you would. I mean, after all, nothing's ever going to be quite the same again, now, is it? Knowing Jeremy has a mistress and baby tucked away somewhere. As you can imagine, Mrs Mullins, I shall be insisting on no less for Jason than your children had – private education, holidays with Jeremy, all that sort of thing – '

'Quite,' I hear myself interrupting. I am still thinking calmly. The impertinence of the girl. The weariness turns into a heavy, physical thing that clouds my whole body.

'So you think it over and I'll ring you back,' she suggests in a bossy voice.

'Oh no, don't ring me back, if you don't mind,' I say, wanting this insane conversation to end, now. I put down the receiver.

The wind still shuffles the curtains. The silence is broken

159

only by the small cracking sounds of the empty chocolate papers as my hand despairs through them in hope of a last one: but no, there are none left. But Jeremy, when he comes early next week, I must now suppose, will not let me down. Jeremy is a loving man. He will bring me new chocolates, lovingly chosen by himself. He is not the sort of man to hurt his wife and family. If there is a complicated side of his life, he will protect us from it. Perhaps he has always done this. Perhaps there have been other . . . complications over the years.

This whole daft matter is, in fact, scarcely worth thinking about, because nothing can ever affect us. The solid base Richenda Gosforth seemed so to envy cannot be disturbed by an outside force. When Jeremy comes, I shall welcome him. He will be pleased to be back, as always. I shall offer him the chocolates he has brought me. He will refuse. We will laugh, exchange news. Naturally, I shall not mention the silly business of Richenda Gosforth's telephone call. I would never dream of intruding in that way. Where there is trust, there is no place for intrusion. I would rather not have known about this squalid girl, of course, but Jeremy will deal with her. He is very competent at sorting out all manner of things. Never will he know, from me, that I know about his son. That is the least a wife can do, keep her silence, if she is to practise her real love for her husband.,

I shall lash out on Monday evening: I shall lash out on turbot and a mousseline sauce, and he'll chide me a little for my extravagance, but really be pleased at the effort I've made. We will have one of our quiet and peaceful evenings together – happy, easy with each other as is our custom. As usual, he will be suffering from jet lag – funny how after flying so many thousands of miles it still affects him – and fall asleep instantly his head touches the pillow. Sometimes I watch his sleeping face for hours. Good, kind, searingly familiar. Oh Jeremy. I think I know you well. I *do* know you well.

Somehow it is nearly midnight. Long past my normal bedtime. In the circumstances, I think I shall treat myself to a mug of hot chocolate and a piece of toast and dripping, the stuff of midnight feasts as a child. Now, standing, in anticipation of such pleasure the weariness has quite fled. I am large and strong and Jeremy's wife. I am warm with trust.

After a while, I go to the kitchen, pour boiling milk into the mug of chocolate powder, and stir the creamy bubbles. I choose a pretty tray for the drink and toast and dripping, and make my way, quite sure of our unchanging love, to bed.

Irish Coffee

*I*t was Magda McCorn's custom to holiday alone. There was not much choice in this matter, but even if there had been she would probably have preferred it that way. She was well acquainted with the many conveniences of the solitary holiday and in the bad moments (which she would scarcely admit to herself, let alone anyone else) remembered to appreciate them.

Last year Mrs McCorn had gone to Sweden. The year before, Norway. Now, she was sick of fish, and twilight afternoons. A yearning for her late husband's country of birth had assailed her one April afternoon, admiring the bilious sweep of King Alfreds in her Cheltenham garden, and within the week she was booked into a first-class hotel in Parknasilla, Co. Kerry.

Mrs McCorn did little at random, and it was only after thorough research that she chose Parknasilla. As her efficient eye swept through the brochures, the name came back to her with a sparkle of nostalgia. It was not her husband, Patrick (born in the shadow of Croagh Patrick, a charming Co. Mayo man), but Commander Chariot, eligible bachelor on a spring cruise to the Canaries some years back, who had recommended the place most warmly. They had been drinking sherry at the ship's bar: the scene was an indelible picture in Mrs McCorn's mind. Commander Chariot wore his panama, despite the overcast skies, while Mrs McCorn had undone the top button of her floral bolero, which would indicate, she felt, a nice distinction between normal reserve and long-term possibility. But if the subtleties of his companion's dress made any impression on the Commander, he did not show it. His bleak grey eyes hovered on the horizon which tilted a little perilously, for Mrs McCorn's sherry-flushed stomach, through the window behind the bar. He chatted on in his charming, impervious way, about Parknasilla (often visited in July) and

165

other places he had enjoyed over the years. All the while calling her Mrs McCorn.

But then the Commander was a not an easy man to get to know. The very first evening aboard, Mrs McCorn, well-trained antennae highly tuned for potential companions, sensed his reserve. Reserve, however, was a challenge rather than a deterrent to the good widow. On many occasions she had found herself quite exhausted from exercising her sympathy on shy fellow holiday-makers and often, as she wore them down, she had recognised the breakthrough, the light, the reward: sometimes it was the offer of a drink or a game of bridge. On other occasions there were confidences, and it was these Mrs McCorn liked best. For in persuading a stranger to 'unwind his soul', as she called it, she felt of some real use, and the satisfaction kindled within her in the bleaker months of the year between holidays.

She had worked very hard upon Commander Chariot, trying to put him at his ease, to draw him from his shell, with the delicate lift of a sympathetic eyebrow, or an almost indistinguishable pat on the arm by her softly padded hand. And indeed, by the last night, amid the coloured rain of paper streamers, she had persuaded him to call her Magda. But she knew he had only complied to her wishes out of politeness. The name had not burst from his lips in a rush of warmth and natural friendliness, and Mrs McCorn had felt disappointed. It was some consolation, of course, to know the other passengers were firmly convinced a shipboard romance had flared between herself and the handsome Commander, and she would not give them any indication that the truth was quite different. She returned to Cheltenham with the Commander's Suffolk address and the promise to 'drop in for a cup of tea if ever she was that way' (which, one day, she would most certainly arrange to be). The Commander made no such promises in return. In a brief farewell, he mentioned – in a voice that was almost callous, Mrs McCorn thought later, considering all the trouble she had taken – that Gloucestershire was not a part of the country he ever had occasion to visit. They did exchange Christmas cards, and Mrs McCorn rather boldly sent postcards from Norway and Sweden – by great strength of will managing to refrain from saying 'Wish you were here'. But her greetings from abroad remained unacknowledged and in terms of *development*, Mrs McCorn was bound to admit, the Commander was a failure.

But hope is often confused with inspiration, and on the journey to Ireland Mrs McCorn could not but help thinking that Fate may have planted the idea of Parknasilla in her head. On the aeroplane she bought herself a small bottle of brandy to quell the feeling of pleasant unease in her stomach: a glittery, excited feeling she had not experienced for many years. But the brandy's medicinal powers had no effect on a state which no medicine can cure, and by the time she set foot on Irish soil Mrs McCorn was as dithery as a girl, her heart a-flutter, her cheeks quite pink.

She walked into the lobby of the Great Southern Hotel mid-afternoon on a fine July day, accompanied by her family of matching suitcases. She moved with head held high, bosom thrust forward, knowing that should her entrance cause a rustle of interest, then those who looked her way would take her for someone. She had persuaded her cautious hairdresser to be a little more generous with the Honey Glow rinse than usual, and by great effort she had lost two pounds through cutting out her elevenses for the last month. She felt she exuded health at this, the beginning of her stay, which is more than can be said of most people, and it was with a symbolic flourish of well being that she signed her name at the reception desk.

Then Magda McCorn, glowing in oatmeal dress with tailored jacket to match, and a butterfly brooch (made from a deceased Red Admiral) sparkling on the lapel, tripped up the wide hotel stairs behind the friendly Irish porter. She admired the high Victorian passages, with their thick and shining white paint, and the ruby carpets. Commander Chariot was a man of taste, of course: he would only recommend the best in hotels. Should he not appear, then at least she would still have benefited from his recommendation and would thank him in a single sentence on the left-hand side of this year's Christmas card.

In her fine room overlooking the bay, the porter relieved himself of all her suitcases and asked if there was anything Mrs McCorn would be requiring. Mrs McCorn paused, smiled, fumbled in her bag for a tip, to give herself time. The only thing in the world she wanted was to know whether Commander Chariot, regular visitor to the Great Southern, was expected. The porter would surely know. But Mrs McCorn was not a woman to indulge in questions that might bring forth a disappointing answer, and after a short, silent struggle, she decided to shake her head and give the man a pound. He could be useful in the future, should she change her mind.

When the porter had gone, Mrs McCorn surveyed what was to be her room for the next two weeks with great satisfaction. Then she went to the window and looked out at the grey waters of the bay. There were palm trees in the hotel garden, reminding her this was a temperate climate and, more distantly, wooded slopes that went down to the sea. I am going to be happy, here, she thought, and sighed at the idea of such a luxury.

Some hours later – having furnished the room with small touches that made it more her own (crochet mat on the bedside table, magazines, travelling clock) – Magda McCorn returned downstairs. It was time to perform her first important task of a holiday: establish her presence. This she did by arming herself with a small glass of sherry, then drifting round the lounges (three of them, with open fires), nodding and smiling with fleeting friendliness in the direction of anyone who caught her glance. The idea was to stamp a firm image in the minds of the other guests: they should instantly understand that here among them was a middle-aged widow of considerable attractions, alone, but in good spirits and certainly not a case for sympathy. While her smile was calculated to indicate enthusiasm, should anyone wish to offer her to join in their conversation or their games, her firm choice of a chair near the window, and apparent engrossment in a book, conveyed also that she was a woman quite happy with her own resources. Her establishing over, her search for the Commander thwarted, Mrs McCorn set about hiding her disappointment in the pages of a light romance.

In the magnificent dining-room of the Great Southern, Mrs McCorn had a single table by the window. There, she enjoyed a four-course dinner cooked by a French chef, and drank half a bottle of expensive claret. Nearby, at other tables, families with children, and several young married couples, chattered their way through the meal. Mrs McCorn did not envy them: it was her joy silently to watch the sun – which put her in mind of a crabapple rather than a tangerine, but then, as Patrick used to say, she was an original thinker – sink into the silver clouds which, if she half shut her eyes, looked like further promontories stretching from the bay. Her measure of wine finished, Mrs McCorn's thoughts took a philosophical turn: the frequent lack of clarity between boundaries (sea and sky, happiness and melancholy) struck her with some hard-to-articulate significance that sent a shiver up her spine. In fact, it had been to Commander Chariot that she had tried to confide some of these private thoughts – as the sun then had been setting over Santa Cruz – but he had shown a lack of response that Mrs McCorn had quite understood. It wasn't everybody who was blessed with such insights, and after all they were of no practical use and the Commander was a wholly practical man.

After dinner, to continue the establishing process, Mrs McCorn made her way to the lounge where the life of the hotel seemed to have gathered. There, an elderly lady wrapped in a mohair shawl, the occasional sequin twinkling in its furry wastes, played the piano. The prime of her piano-playing years was evidently over and, accompanied by a dolorous young man on the double bass, their rendering of fifties tunes lacked spirit. It was as if the music was emerging from under a huge, invisible cushion, oppressed. But it was good enough for Mrs McCorn. In her time she had had quite a reputation on the dance floor, although partnering her husband Patrick there had been little opportunity to show off her prowess at the quickstep. It would have been disloyal to complain, and she never did: although for all the happyish years of their marriage, Magda McCorn secretly deplored the fact that her husband was such a lout on the dance floor. But her feeling for the dance, as she called it, never left her and here, suddenly as of old, she felt her toes privately wiggling in her patent pumps in time to the steady thump of 'Hey, there! You with the Stars in Your Eyes' which, she recalled with a stab of nostalgia, had been played every night on the cruise to the Canaries.

Mrs McCorn chose herself a tactful armchair. That is, it was within reach of a middle-aged Norwegian couple, should they

169

choose to talk to her: yet far enough away to make ignoring her within the bounds of politeness if that was how they felt. She gave them a small signalling smile and was delighted, though not surprised, when immediately they drew their own chairs closer to hers and began to converse in beautiful English.

Due to her holiday in Norway, Mrs McCorn was able to tell them many interesting things about their country, and to captivate their interest for some time. Occasionally she allowed her eyes to glance at the dance floor, where she observed the deplorable sight of unmusical men shunting around their wives with not the slightest regard to the beat of the tune. The long-suffering expressions of the wives did not escape her, either. She felt for them, poor dears, and envied them, too. Varicose veins a-twinkle, at least they were on their feet.

Something of her feelings must have registered in Mrs McCorn's eyes, for the Norwegian gentlemen was standing, offering her his arm, asking her to dance. Taken so unawares, Mrs McCorn hardly knew whether to accept or refuse. But she saw the friendly smile of the Norwegian wife urging her, urging her, and knowing everything would be above board, with the clinical Norwegian eyes of the wife following their every move, Mrs McCorn said yes.

On the small floor, they lumbered round in imitation of a foxtrot. Mrs McCorn, confident that the delicate tracery on the back of her own calves was well hidden by her Dusky Sunbeam tights, gave a small shake of her hips to encourage her partner.

'You dance very well,' this spurred him to say, and Mrs McCorn began to enjoy herself. Should Commander Chariot come in now, he could not fail to observe the way in which people were drawn to her wherever she went, and surely he would be moved to admiration.

Mrs McCorn's two-week holiday passed happily enough. She befriended many of the other guests in the hotel, and every evening found herself in the desirable position of joining in games, drinks and conversations. Her new acquaintances included many foreigners, and Mrs McCorn was able to let the fact be known that she was a much-travelled woman herself, for all her quiet life in Cheltenham – with quite a flair for

Continental cooking and with some talent for making herself understood in French.

The pounds of flesh that Mrs McCorn had so industriously lost before coming to Ireland were soon regained, and indeed increased, by her indulgence in the delicious food. But Mrs McCorn did not care.

Realising that Fate had slipped up and been unkind in its choice of dates, and there was little hope Commander Chariot would appear, she sought consolation in cooked breakfasts in bed (beautifully arranged trays, flat grey water unblinking in the bay outside her window), hearty lunches and enormous dinners. But as her plumpness did nothing to diminish her evident popularity, so she saw no reason for cutting back until she returned home.

On the last day of her visit, Mrs McCorn – who for the most part had spent sedentary days – decided to join a trip to the Skellig Islands. She was all for a little adventure, and felt the breath of sea air would be of benefit to her complexion.

It dawned a disappointingly grey and misty day, a light drizzle swirling so weightless through the air you could not see it all. Mrs McCorn contemplated abandoning the trip, but then felt that would be faint-hearted, and cheered herself with the thought that Irish weather was wonderfully changeable, and at any moment the sun might drive away the cloud.

And indeed, by the time she was seated snugly in her poplin mackintosh and silk scarf on the fishing boat, along with some dozen foreign students, the gloom had begun to lift and the sun threw a first pale rope of light along the horizon. Mrs McCorn did not much like the bucking motion of the boat as it lumbered over the waves, but she sucked on her boiled sweets and concentrated on the feeling of enjoying the proximity to young foreigners. Widening her horizons, she was, she felt. Perhaps before the day was over she would find the chance to make herself known to them, although for the moment she could detect no openings. They were a dour lot: unwashed, unshaven, dirty clothes and unhealthy skin. But then Mrs McCorn, who was sensitive to the hardships of those less fortunate than herself, supposed they could not afford to live on anything but fish and chips on their camping holiday, and was not surprised. She could have wished they had appeared friendlier, more willing to talk: a little conversation would have been agreeable, but perhaps they kept their interest for monuments rather than people.

After an hour of bumping over the grey sea, Mrs McCorn and the other sightseers were rewarded by the sight of the first island. It loomed out of the misty sea like a single tooth. The fanciful thought came to Mrs McCorn that the whole Atlantic Ocean was a vast, grey tongue, hissing and snapping and drooling with white-spittle foam, armed with its one hideous giant tooth. And the sky was a grim upper lip. The vast and dreadful mouth, made from the elements, only waited for the right time to swallow the boat-load with a single flick of its lapping tongue . . . Mrs McCorn sucked harder on her raspberry drop and listened to the wail of forty thousand gannets, who fluttered round their island thickly as a snowstorm. Occasionally one of them would swoop quite close to the boat, dismissing the passengers with its beady red eye, then diving into the waves to snap at an invisible fish.

The second island, their destination, came into sight. It was another monster rock, sheer and black and menacing. Waves thundered round its base, thousands more gulls screamed their indignation at having to live in such a God-forsaken spot. It was here that seven hundred years ago a small band of monks chose to build a monastery on its summit. To climb hundreds of steps to see the remains of this monastery was the aim of the expedition.

The boat moored at a small concrete pier. Mrs McCorn looked about her in dismay. She had imagined it would be quite primitive, of course: a simple tea shop, perhaps, and a small cluster of cottages. But there was nothing. The petulant gulls were the only inhabitants, balancing on the edges of precarious rock nests, screaming all the while. Close to, the rock was no less intimidating. While the waves pounded upwards, other water streamed down the jagged sides, gleaming, oily. Mrs McCorn was afraid.

Gritting her teeth, remembering she was British, she followed the students up the dangerous little flight of steps. There, they abandoned her with peculiar speed, scampering up the steep path with an eagerness Mrs McCorn found herself unable to share. She followed them slowly, tucking the lunch

172

box the hotel had given her under one arm, and telling herself she must persevere, however undesirable the climb may seem.

Although Mrs McCorn's progress was very slow – students from another boat passed her with uncaring speed – she soon became out of breath and listened to her own panting against the dimmer noise of waves thudding far below. She was forced to conclude that she should have to rest before the top, or she might risk a heart attack. And who, then . . .? She chose a small, flat rock at the edge of steps, sat down, and unbuttoned her mackintosh. The hotel had provided her with an unimaginative lunch, but she found comfort in the sliced-bread sandwiches, tomatoes, biscuits and cheese. Her breathing returned to its normal pace, and after a while she began to feel cool again.

When she had finished eating, Mrs McCorn looked about for somewhere to bury her empty lunch box. There were no litter bins, of course, and the sea was much too far away to throw the wretched thing over the edge. Mrs McCorn scrabbled about the springy green stuff that grew among the rocks, and eventually managed, by squishing it quite small, to hide the box. Plunging her hands into the greenery gave her a nasty turn: its cold sliminess was surprising. But she completed the job to her satisfaction, and turned for another look at the bewildering expanse of grey Atlantic before continuing on her way.

The sky was whitish-grey, mists swirled blotchily about the sheer sides of rock. In the distance, the sea kept up its perpetual snarl, and the gulls their angry screeching. Mrs McCorn had never felt so alone. To lift her spirits, she thought of the ordinary things of her life: her small, neat garden, her well-Hoovered carpets, her Silver Jubilee tin of biscuits, always full, in the kitchen, her cat Tibby, the absolute regularity of the Parish Newsletter – things which sometimes she found lacking in excitement, but which now she appreciated with all her heart. Then, for the first time that day, she thought of Commander Chariot.

As she did so, Mrs McCorn stood up. No point in dwelling on the unlikely, she thought, and at that moment a small chink of sun appeared in the sky, making the wet rocks glint. An omen, thought Mrs McCorn, and at once forced herself to abandon the idea as silly. But, trudging slowly up the rough steps once more, she could not cast aside the Commander. He filled her being in an unaccountable way: she longed for his presence. With him this day on the island would be an agreeable adventure, instead of the frightening experience it was in reality. Alive in her mind, the Commander then spoke to Mrs McCorn in a voice so real he might have been at her side.

'Ruddy masochists, those monks must have been,' he said ('ruddy' was his favourite adjective), and Mrs McCorn smiled.

Somehow, she got to the top. It was no great reward. A cluster of stone-built cells, gently rounded structures, putting Mrs McCorn in mind of house martins' nests. Very uncomfortable, they must have been, with their slit windows and damp floors, the mists and rain flurrying about outside, and nothing to comfort in the sight of the grim Atlantic sea. Mrs McCorn ventured into one of the cells: it smelt wet and spooky. When her eyes had grown accustomed to the dark, she noticed three of the students sitting on the floor in a corner. They passed an evil-smelling cigarette between them, and gave her an unfriendly look. Mrs McCorn hurried out.

She was quite cold by now, and thought with longing of the hotel bath and her warm candlewick dressing-gown. Only a few more hours . . . And it would, of course, be a good story to tell friends at home, not that she'd ever be up to describing the strange sense of horror that the island of rock had given her.

Before returning to the path to descend, Mrs McCorn leaned over one of the ruined stone walls and looked down, down at the spumy sea battering for ever the base of the rock, and she listened to the endless evil screeching of the gulls. It was then it came to her why the silly old monks had chosen such a place to live: they had wanted to confront the devil head-on and this was the perfect spot. There was no grain of comfort, of soft or easy living on the rock land or the monster sea. The gannets were devils incarnate, the brief flashes of sun a simple mockery. On this island was the rough face of God – quite unlike the God Mrs McCorn was acquainted with in the church at Cheltenham with its carpeted aisle and central heating. On

174

this island, you'd have to be tougher than she, Mrs McCorn, to go on believing.

Physically weakened by such thoughts, and by the day's exposure to relentless elements, Mrs McCorn put the last of the boiled sweets in her mouth and began her slow descent. She found her knees were shaking and she was sweating quite hard into her poplin mackintosh. But for all the loneliness, she was glad there was no one here to witness the way in which the island had unnerved her – that is, except for Commander Chariot. He would have scoffed at any talk of devils and talked knowledgeably of the breeding habits of gannets, which would have been very cheering. As it was, he was far from Ireland, or this place, with no thought of her. Mrs McCorn shuffled down the steps, one foot always forward like a small child, praying for the bottom.

Three hours later, in the safety of her hotel room, Mrs McCorn, although much happier, still found herself somewhat shaken. She packed her suitcase, so as to be ready for her departure in the morning, and it took her twice as long as usual. In her confusion she found she had put soft things at the bottom, and had to start all over again.

As it was her last night, Mrs McCorn felt it unnecessary to make quite the same effort she had made on previous evenings. She wore her plainest dress – very tight, now, across the stomach – and brushed half-heartedly at the mess the Skellig Islands had made of her hair. Somehow, she couldn't face drinks in the lounge – no energy, as yet, to recount the adventure of her day. She waited in her room until eight o'clock, then went straight into the dining-room.

She saw him at once. Commander Chariot was sitting at the window at a single table next to her own. Mrs McCorn's instant thought was to flee – to unpack her turquoise Lurex and change into that, and to have another go at her hair. But she was too late. He had seen her. He smiled, slightly.

Mrs McCorn followed the waiter to her table. She sat down and quickly ordered her dinner and half a bottle of wine. Then she allowed herself to look at the Commander, who was halfway through a plate of elaborate chops.

'Why, hello there, Mrs McCorn,' he said.

'Magda,' she said, with warmth and humour.

'Well I never, running into you here of all places.'

'It was your recommendation, you may remember.'

'Was it? Was it, now? Can't say I do remember. Anyhow, here for long, are you?'

Mrs McCorn gave herself time to think before answering. Perhaps it would be possible to make new arrangements after dinner, to extend her stay for a few days. But there was the question of money (she had spent every penny of her holiday budget) and getting another flight back – too many complications.

'I'm leaving tomorrow morning, actually,' she said.

'Well, well, what a ruddy shame.'

The Commander hustled a forkful of cauliflower into his mouth, shifting his eyes. His expression just might have been one of relief.

But this paranoid thought was quickly dispelled from Mrs McCorn's mind by the next turn of events: the Commander suggested he might join her at her table, seeing as they would have only one evening together.

Scarcely able to believe her good fortune, Mrs McCorn signalled to the waiter. He moved the Commander's place to Mrs McCorn's table, picked up the bottle of wine, and lifted an eyebrow at Mrs McCorn. Her heart thumping, Mrs McCorn nodded. The waiter poured the Commander a glass of the wine: the Commander did not protest.

Outside, there was an orange sky over the bay, and a small hard gold sun. Mrs McCorn wondered if she should put to the Commander her funny idea about a *crabapple* sun. But she thought better of it, and said instead:

'It's been quite a few years, hasn't it? And you haven't changed at all.'

'No. Well. I manage to keep myself up to scratch.'

Indeed, it was true he had not changed: no more grey hairs, no new wrinkles, the same handsome combination of angular bone and fine-drawn skin. Mrs McCorn found herself gazing at him in wonder and in disbelief. The only pity was the cruel timing. But she would not let herself think of the sadness of

176

the morning. There was the whole night: time in which to play her cards with skill.

To keep a clear head, Mrs McCorn let the Commander drink all her wine, and ordered him another bottle. She delighted in his pleasure in the stuff: the way he sipped and swirled and sniffed with such expertise. They talked of their various trips, and the Commander acknowledged her cards from Norway and Sweden.

'I'm so glad they reached you. I thought that maybe – you know the foreign posts.'

'Oh, I *got* them all right. Should have written back, but I'm not much of a dab hand when it comes to letters myself.'

'I know just how you feel.' (This was a permissible lie. Mrs McCorn had no idea, as a great letter- and postcard-writer herself, how it must feel not to have the constant desire to keep in touch.)

By the end of dinner, the Commander had a bright pink spot on both cheeks (crabapples, again, thought Mrs McCorn). He was friendly and seemingly happy, but not exactly lively. There were long pauses between each comment he made, and the comments themselves were not of the stuff that remains for ever in the romantic memory. Mrs McCorn, remembering his long monologues about fishing and the Navy, wondered if there was anything troubling him. Given the right moment, she felt she should make a gentle enquiry.

'It's really quite lively here, evenings,' she said. 'Shall we take our coffee in the lounge?'

The Commander followed. She led the way as far as the quiet room where the less lively guests read their papers round the fire, and the Commander indicated they should occupy the free sofa. But Mrs McCorn shook her head determinedly, and kept going till she reached two vacant chairs at the side of the dance floor. With a look of barely concealed pain on his face, as if the pianist's rendering of 'Stardust' hurt his ears, the Commander lowered himself into one of the chairs. Mrs McCorn, meantime, was smiling and waving to nearby friends in some triumph: they had all heard about her friendship with the Commander, and to be with him on this, her last night, was a proud occasion. So engrossed was she in acknowledging the waves and smiles – yet at the same time not wanting to encourage anyone to draw so near as to deflect the Commander's interest from herself – she was quite unaware that her own choice of seat was disagreable to her companion. With the elation of a girl, she summoned the waiter.

'Let's be devils, shall we, Commander, and treat ourselves to Irish coffees?'

She knew, even as she made the suggestion, the treat would be put on her bill, and she did not care. What did strike her, with a brief iciness of heart, was her own word *devil*. She remembered the lugubrious island of evil gulls she had so recently visited. But the dreadful experience seemed wonderfully far away, now. She was back where she belonged, in a place of warmth and sentimental tunes and safety.

The Irish coffees came. Mrs McCorn sat back, revelling in the warm froth on her top lip as she sipped the sickly drink, one foot tapping the floor in time to the music. In truth, it would have been hard to have a conversation against the noise of the band, and the Commander, Mrs McCorn observed, was sunk in that pleasurable silence that is permitted between those of understanding. The broad-hipped dancers swayed about, sometimes giving their bodies a small flick, to show some vestige of youth still lived under the middle-aged clothes.

Mrs McCorn prayed the Commander would ask her to take the floor, to join them, to *show* them, but he did no such thing. And despite her vague sympathies for women's liberation, she felt it would not be quite the thing to make the proposal herself. She waved airily at one of the dancers, disguising her disappointment.

'I've made a lot of friends here,' she said. Commander Chariot nodded. They had a second Irish coffee. The Commander, making much of his gallantry, paid with a lot of small change out of his pocket. The pianist struck up, by wonderful chance, 'Hey there! You with the Stars in Your Eyes'. Mrs McCorn could restrain herself no longer.

'Do you remember, Commander?' she asked. 'Our tune? On the cruise?'

The Commander looked at her blankly. 'Can't say I do. Music's all the same to me. Wouldn't mind if I never heard another note in my life.'

Her ploy having failed, Mrs McCorn ordered two further

glasses of Irish coffee – the Commander made no attempt, this time, to pay – so that he should not be aware of the deflation she felt.

They spent the next hour drinking Irish coffee, unspeaking, except to agree to another order. By eleven o'clock, Mrs McCorn felt both reckless and sick. The Commander, she noticed, had a cluster of sweat on both temples, and was flushed. Time, she thought.

'Well, I must be turning in, Commander. Early start tomorrow, for the plane.'

Her words sounded thick as whipped cream. The Commander heaved himself up out of the deep chair and helped her to her feet.

'Jolly good idea,' he said.

Very slowly, Mrs McCorn made her way to the stairs. The pillars through which she threaded her way spun like acrobats' plates. When she tried to smile at various friends, her mouth slithered about in an uncontrollable way, and the feeling of nausea increased. But at last she achieved the foot of the stairs, and felt the mahogany bannister solid beneath her liquid hand. She paused, turned carefully to the Commander, whose eyes were at half-mast, and whose mouth sagged.

'So it's *au revoir*, but not goodbye,' she slurred.

'*Au revoir* but not goodbye.' The Commander, too, held on to the bannister, his hand only an inch away from Mrs McCorn's. The repetition of her own words gave her courage: in the floundering feather globe of her mind, she realised it was her last chance.

'Nightcap, Commander? Just a small one?'

A long pause. 'Why not?' answered the Commander eventually.

They negotiated the stairs, climbing each one as if it was a separate challenge, drifted like slurry along the moving ruby carpet to Mrs McCorn's room. There, the Commander dropped at once into the velvet armchair. Mrs McCorn hastily hid her peach Dacron nightie – nicely laid out by the maid – under the pillow, and telephoned for two more Irish coffees.

In her own room, she felt better. The sickness seemed to have passed, her head rocked rather than span. The coffees came. Once more, she and the Commander plunged their mouths into the comforting warm froth of cream, and sipped, without speaking. Mrs McCorn lost all sense of time. Her legs felt as if they were cast in swan's-down, her heart beat wildly as it had in all her imaginings of this climactic scene, and she realised it was no longer possible to continue her life without the Commander.

The next thing she knew she was on the floor by his chair (one shoe had fallen off), her hands running up his trouser legs. A strange moaning came from her lips.

'Commander! Commander! You are my life, I am your slave, your obedient servant, your slave for ever!'

She was dimly aware of her crescendoing voice, and the Commander's bony fingers trying to unlatch her hands from his grey flannel thighs.

'Get off, Mrs McCorn! Get *up*, Mrs McCorn! Don't be so ruddy stupid.'

Through the humming in Mrs McCorn's ears, he sounded as if he meant to be stern, but the words lacked vigour.

'How can you say such cruel things to one who is your life, to one who has waited for you like Patience on a – '

'Get *up*, I say, Mrs McCorn. You're ruining the creases in my trousers.'

Mrs McCorn rose awkwardly as a zeppelin, poised above him for the merest second, then dropped on to his outspread knees, curling into a foetal position. Before he had time to protest, she had grabbed his jaw in one of her hands, squeezed his mouth into an open hole, and thrust her creamy lips on to his. For a blissful moment, she managed to taste *his* Irish coffee and feel the small points of his teeth. She heard him moan, and lashed his tongue more wildly. But then she felt vicious fingers in her ribs, and drew back, crying out with pain.

'Get off, you silly old baggage! What the ruddy hell do you think you're doing?'

'Magda! Call me Magda . . .'

'I'll call the manager. Rape!'

The word struck Mrs McCorn like a blade. She unfurled herself, holding the sore ribs. Stood.

'You don't understand, Commander.'

'I understand only too well, Mrs McCorn.'

'You've taken this all wrong.'

'You're blind drunk and disgusting with it.'

Somehow the words had little impact. They fell on Mrs McCorn's ears without wounding, but she felt it was incumbent upon her to protest.

'Commander! That's no way to speak when all I wanted – '

'I'm getting out of here.'

The Commander rose. His mouth was smeared with Mrs McCorn's Amber Fire lipstick, his sparse hair stood up in spikes. She felt sorry for him. He looked wounded, misunderstood. Mrs McCorn would have liked to have put a gentle hand on his head, smooth the hair, and say, There, there, it's all right now: it's all over. But she resisted.

The Commander moved to the door. He seemed both cowed and fed up.

'I'm sorry if I caused you any offence, Mrs McCorn,' he said quietly, in his normal voice, 'but a man has to protect himself from attack.'

'Quite.' Mrs McCorn nodded. She would have agreed to anything at that moment.

'And I realise you were overcome. Not yourself.'

'I'm sorry. Quite overcome. Not myself at all.'

'Well, I've survived worse things at sea.'

Gentleman to the last, thought Mrs McCorn.

'And now I must go to bed. You're not the only one with an early start. Tomorrow I'm off on a trip to the Skellig Islands.' He reached for the door knob.

Mrs McCorn had been aware of her spirits rising as the Commander made his apology. All was not lost. But with this fresh, final piece of news, they fell to a place so deep within her she had not previously been aware of its existence.

'The Skellig Islands?'

'Always wanted to go there. Well, goodnight.'

He left very quickly. When he had gone, Mrs McCorn fell back on to the bed. Too weak to analyse the failure of the evening, too disheartened even to chide herself, she cried for a while, and then fell asleep.

The maid who brought her breakfast found her next morning, still dressed, on top of the bed, one shoe still on, make-up awry. Somehow, Mrs McCorn roused herself and overcame this little embarrassment with considerable dignity, and even a joke about the effects of Irish coffee. Then she hastened to repair herself, and finish her packing.

Downstairs, she looked about for the Commander, but then she remembered the time of her own departure to the Skelligs yesterday and realised he would already have gone. When she was given the bill, she smiled at the huge sum the Irish coffees had amounted to, and with soft gentle fingers touched the headache that braided her forehead. Various friends from the hotel were there to see her off, and said how much she would be missed. Their declarations touched Mrs McCorn: at least she had made an impression in some quarters.

On the aeroplane over the Irish Sea, she found herself imagining the Commander retracing her own steps of yesterday, or a million years ago, or whenever the thoroughly nasty day had been. But she imagined *he* was enjoying it, and she admired him for that. He was a man of vision in some ways but, unused to much contact with women, could be sympathised with for not recognising true worth when he saw it. Her conclusions about the Commander thus neatly parcelled in her mind, Mrs McCorn searched in her bag for a boiled sweet. And as the coast of England, dear England, came into sight, she decided that on this year's Christmas card she would simply add, Did you enjoy the Skelligs? Thereafter would follow months in which she could look forward to an answer, and life in Cheltenham would continue to be lived in hope.

Not for Publication

*D*iscipline as usual, today. Doubt if anything short of another war could make me change my routine now. Old men get stuck in their ways, haven't the heart to change them.

Grey sky, slight wind, leaves beginning to turn. I eagerly read the weather first thing every morning. A fine day makes me look forward to the afternoon walk, though I don't mind rain. I'd never retire to a hot climate. Seven thirty: open the kitchen door for Jacob. He lumbers out into the orchard, squashing autumn crocuses with every step, the old bugger. Careless, but affectionate, is Jacob. Make myself a piece of toast – can't be bothered with a boiled egg these days – and a cup of tea. Put knife and plate into the sink, run the tap. Mrs Cluff says, 'You leave it, General, till I come.' But I don't like to. I like to do my bit.

Jacob returns, muddy paws. 'You brute, Jacob,' I say. He wags his tail. The most intelligent dogs have their soppy side. He follows me to the study. Goes straight to his place under the desk. The high point of Jacob's day is our walk on the Common after lunch. He knows this will be his reward for patience during my morning stint at the typewriter. He's learned the best way to get through the hours is to sleep. He sleeps.

I light the electric fire. Real fire in the evenings, when Mrs Cluff has done the grate. I lower myself into my creaky old chair (presented to me, at my request and much to their amazement, by my fellow officers when I retired. Well, I'd enjoyed sitting in it for so many years).

I glance out at the clouds behind the apple tree. Can just see a distant hill. It's not like my native Yorkshire, here. But not a bad bit of country. Tame.

I pick up *The Times*. I allow myself fifteen minutes to read it each morning, then begin writing at nine on the dot. 'Start when you *mean* to start,' my Commanding Officer used to say. I always try to take his advice. He was a sound man.

I'm having a bash at my memoirs. Military, mostly. I had a good war. Nothing personal, of course. Don't go along with all this exposure of private life in memoirs, myself. I was horrified only yesterday to see that some tinkering American professor had pried further than any previous biographer into Jane Austen's brief and innocent engagement to one Harris Bigg-Wither. (Imagine: *Pride and Prejudice* by Jane Bigg-Wither. Wouldn't have been the same at all.) Let her keep her secret to herself, I say. Stop nosing about. How will it further our knowledge and pleasure in her work to know that Miss Austen and Mr B-W held hands? Her secret should be allowed to rest peacefully with her in her grave.

Anyhow. I don't imagine anyone will want to read my story, let alone publish it. But I keep at it. Can't do nothing but garden in retirement. Have to keep exercising the old brain. Besides, one or two of the family might be interested once I'm dead. They never care to listen to me much in life.

I put on my specs. Telephone rings. Dammit. Very unusual. Not many people ring me these days and those who do are of the economical kind, won't lift a receiver before six o'clock.

'Hello? Gerald?'

Petronella – my sister. Petronella is a bossy, interfering, loud-voiced and large woman. She lives in Petworth and swanks about Sussex. She's married to a boring husband in commodities, and has four exceptionally dull and tiresome grown-up children married to suitably dull –

'Yes?'

'Seen *The Times*?'

'Not yet.'

'Despatches,' she snaps.

'Who?'

Not Laurence, I hope. My oldest friend, Laurence, in a Home near Folkestone. Been meaning to ring him . . .

'You look. Old friend of yours's husband.'

She gives a barking laugh, slams down the receiver. Petronella has always been of the mistaken belief that not to say goodbye lends a woman mystery. Silly cow.

Relief it's not old Laurence, though. I find the Deaths column. Eyes slip down. Bit slow, bit nervous.

Macdunnald, Vaughan Robert. Peacefully in his sleep after a long illness. Couple of days ago.

So, Mrs Vaughan Macdunnald, Mary Macdunnald, is a widow. That's what that means.

Mary, Mary, Mary Jay.

I put my hands flat on the desk, steady myself. *Brace up, General, greet the morning.* 'Don't hurry over the weighing up,' my Commanding Officer used to say – sound man, admirable fellow – 'then make the decision *snappy*.' His barking voice in my ears. I shut my eyes. Prepare to obey. *This, being something of a special day, dear Lord, forgive me for abandoning the military side of my memoirs this morning . . .*

The winter of 1947, you may remember, was cursed with some of the worst snow of the century. I had recently moved in here, and pretty primitive it was, too: no heating, hot water on the blink, garden a jungle. I had bought it for its potential, but was uncertain how to proceed with the transformation. What it needed was the hand of some imaginative woman. As it was, it took me some time to get the place shipshape with the help of a solitary builder. That first winter was pretty grim. I had to sleep in my greatcoat, chip ice off the windows every morning. I was grateful to have only a few days' leave at a time.

Still, I did have a woman vaguely in mind. Veronica. We met at a dinner dance given by Laurence – who's very rich – to cheer his remaining friends after the war. It wasn't much of an occasion by today's standards: food pretty drab, rationed clothes not up to much. But we enjoyed ourselves. Veronica and I took the floor for several quicksteps, and a fast waltz to end the evening. I was quite a dancer in my day, could see she was impressed. I gave her a lift home to a mansion block in Victoria. She talked about Byron. She had quite a thing about Byron. 'Brains as well as a good looker,' Laurence said.

Few weeks later, I took her to lunch at Browns Hotel. More Byron. She drank lemon barley which she said was a real treat. Not a bad girl, not bad at all. On the big side, but friendly.

Back here in the cottage, I allowed myself to weave a few fantasies about Veronica. She'd be the right sort to bring a house alive, I thought. And good, child-bearing hips. I spent a few sleepless nights – the cold, to be honest, more than the thought of Veronica. After a week or so, I decided to make the next move.

Another evening at the Savoy? I suggested. Where we met, after all, I said, thinking I'd have a stab at a show of romance. The idea went down very well. We planned to meet the next Friday evening. I would be in a black tie. She would be in a long blue dress.

That afternoon, I trudged through the snow to the village (not deep enough, then, to deter my gallant old Wolseley from getting to London) with Ralphie (Jacob's ancestor) at my side. I exchanged many saved-up coupons for a box of chocolates, and began to anticipate the evening with considerable pleasure.

I set off in plenty of time, punctuality being my byword. It had begun to snow again, lightly, and was bitterly cold. But the Wolseley started with its beautiful, reassuring purr. I drove cautiously down the lane, windscreen wipers doing their best against the dark flakes. A full moon, there was, I remember. In two hours I would be with Veronica in the warmth of the Savoy.

The snow fell more thickly. After three miles, the car whimpered to a halt. I tried everything, but the engine was completely dead. Snow piled up quickly on the bonnet. By a stroke of luck, I was fifty yards from my friends, Arthur and Janet Knight, both doctors. They lived in a farmhouse set a little back from the place in which I had come to a halt. Nothing else for it: I must call upon them for help.

Janet opened the door, light from the hall gushed on to the slippery step where I stood. She looked in amazement at my black tie and snow-covered greatcoat. Behind her, packing cases rose almost to the ceiling: she and Arthur were leaving for a spell in Canada the following week.

'Gerald! Whatever – ? Come on in.'

The door shut behind me. The warmth of their house lapped up at me like a welcoming animal. Arthur came hurrying out.

188

I explained the problem. He responded with absolute conviction.

'Tell you what: give up. It's not the night to try to get a car going, and with the snow getting worse it'd be daft to try to get to London. Ring your date, tell her what's happened, and stay to dinner with us. There's plenty of rabbit stew and we need someone to entertain a friend of ours.'

The suggestion was practical, tempting. Before I could protest, my coat was taken from me and I was hustled into the sitting-room, a cosy, dingy room with a huge inglenook fireplace. Logs shifted beneath lively flames. Dense shadows, out of the fire's reach, confused my eyes for a moment. There was a distinct smell of apples – I observed a plate of lustreless Bramleys sitting on a bookshelf – and lavender. Bunches of the stuff, dried, were laid by the fire. Sitting near them, on a low stool, was the Knights' friend, Mary Jay.

She was quite small, I noticed at once, with a pale serious face, devoid of make-up, and huge brown eyes. She wore a dull brown dress of some wollen stuff, the colour of milk chocolate. It had a prim lace collar. Rather Lyons Corner House waitressy, I thought, as she stood up to shake hands.

Janet introduced me as Colonel Arlington. Mary smiled – a smile so slow, so contained, so enchanting that I felt the huge mass of my hand tremble as I briefly held hers. Then she sat down again, huddling her arms round her knees, as if my entrance had done nothing to interrupt her daydream.

In the forty years since that evening, I must have gone over every word, every look, every moment, a million times. With the assumption of old age (I hesitate to call it wisdom) I now understand that there are moments in our lives when some being within us craves something so amorphous it is not strictly definable, but the force of craving puts us into a state of readiness to receive. I believe that is how it must have been, for me, that night. After a life of almost chaste bachelorhood, I longed for something not yet experienced, the warmth of a fellow spirit, the notion of giving everything I had to a fellow creature. Veronica, I knew, was irrelevant to my search. To her, I made conventional overtures with a kind of vague, unanalysed sense of duty, but with no conviction.

In my state of readiness, perhaps, any woman who had been

189

sitting by the Knights' fire that evening might have had the same impact upon me as did Mary. But I think not. It's impossible to imagine another woman igniting such devastating, instant effect. I felt ill, cold, terrified.

As a fighting soldier, I had lived so recently with daily fear, was accustomed to its manifestations: freezing blood, disobedient limbs, loosening bowels. I had learned how to switch on the automatic button in the brain that commands the body to go forth in strength, in faith, with calm. I had learned, as a leader of men, the necessity to inspire courage in others by disguising one's own fear in a guise of courage. Looking down at that small, still woman in her brown dress, I felt more afraid than on any battlefield. Here was someone who was about to change my life. (Ah, little then did I ever guess how.) I was giddy, weak, confused by the total unexpectedness of this break in my journey, by flames replacing snow, by warmth instead of cold. My heart was beating like a wild thing because of the presence of this stranger; had I reached the Savoy, it would have remained quite regular on the dance floor. I sat on a chair as far from Mary as I could manage. I hoped she would not be able to observe me well in the shadows.

Arthur went off to ring the garage, Janet to get me a drink. Mary Jay and I were left listening to the fire. I didn't feel there was any need to speak, but then I heard my own voice, all awry, blurting out some mindless comment.

'That dress you're wearing,' I said. 'It's the colour of a Mars Bar, isn't it?' Did my voice sound as peculiar to her as it did to me? 'Not my favourite colour,' I added, cursing myself as the words escaped.

What devil made me say such a thing, so rudely, to a woman I'd met just two minutes ago? Was it self-defence, resenting the shock she had caused me? Mary swivelled round to face me, fingering the stuff of the skirt, smiling slightly again.

'I know. It's pretty awful, isn't it? I was trying to find a real chestnut. But you know what it's like, still. No choice. Nothing.'

'I'm sorry.' I was wringing my hands. 'That was terribly rude of me. I don't know what – '

She looked at me as if she really did not mind, perhaps hadn't even noticed.

'That's all right. I like people to say what they think, don't you?'

And those huge brown eyes, each sparkling with a minuscule candle of flame from the fire, looked straight into my soul.

Arthur returned. Mary and I both shifted our positions. Arthur noticed nothing untoward, which was strange: I could have sworn the recognition between Mary and me was tangible, visible to the naked eye. The garage would fetch the car in the morning, snow permitting. Hadn't I better ring . . . ? suggested Arthur.

Lumbering to the telephone in the hall, I felt as if each step was pushing against a heavy sea, so great was my reluctance to move. But the good soldier within me explained with military precision the situation to Veronica. She was very nice about it, quite understood. I said I would be in touch, knowing this was not true. What was the point of Veronica, now Mary . . .? Janet put a large whisky and soda into my hand.

We ate bowls of rabbit stew round the fire, the kitchen being too cold. I asked no questions, but learned that Mary, whose home was in the Borders, was staying in The Black Swan, a small hotel near Henley. She was a painter, it seemed, but the purpose of her visit was not explained. She was here tonight to say farewell to the Knights before their departure for Canada. Janet was an old schoolfriend.

Our supper finished – an excellent sago pudding with tinned greengages and a small piece of Cheddar followed the rabbit – Arthur put Schubert's 'Trout' on the gramophone. Mary was still on her low stool, arms huddled round her knees again. The rest of us lay back in our armchairs, listening. I positioned myself so that she should not see me watching her. In that room as warm as fur, the musical water twinkled as never before, while the trout leapt, irrepressible, against calmer flames of the fire. My eyes never left the small, still shape of Mary, with her downcast lashes.

At eleven, this bewitching woman looked at her watch. She offered me a lift home, assured me that her Austin Seven would not let us down. It was on her way, she said. Had my head been clearer, I would have realised at once that my path lay in quite the opposite direction to Henley.

Mary wrapped a long scarf round her neck, put on a huge

191

coat, woolly hat and gloves. Her farewells to her friends the Knights were prolonged. Mine were grateful, but brief. Still unsure of my voice, I was, and distracted by the glorious sensations searing through my body.

The Austin Seven was very small inside, but gallant. It snuffled through the deep snow, wonderfully slow. Mary concentrated on her driving. We did not speak. I concentrated on her profile – what there was left of it, between hat and scarf – the delicately tipped nose, the short curling upper lip pursed in concentration, and giving no hint of the smiles it contained. The sky was clear, but dark as those blackout nights when people crouched in shelters waiting for the siren to howl All Clear. It had stopped snowing. There was an infinite arc of stars above us, and a powerful moon. Its light encased Mary's side view in a glittering frame. Every strand of escaped hair was visible, iridescent as cobweb threads. The fluffed outline of her childlike hat sparkled richly as silver fox fur.

At my gate, all too soon, I congratulated my driver. Congratulations! How steeped we are in convention: how it props us, clumsily, in heightened moments. So inappropriate, my congratulations in the midnight snow: would I had a poet's art of the right word. But again, she didn't seem to mind.

'Oh, it was nothing. I'm used to such conditions. Scotland . . .'

She smelled of sugared violets, the sweet iced cakes of childhood.

'I won't ask you in,' I said.

'No,' she said. 'I must be getting back.'

'It's perishing, when my fire's out.'

I felt I owed her some kind of explanation in case she was the sort of girl accustomed to being offered late-night champagne.

'I can imagine.' Her small smile snapped the last thread of my discretion.

'How long are you here for?' I asked.

'Another week, perhaps.'

'Would you like – well, lunch or something, one day?'

She hestitated. Then she said, Yes, that would be nice, and I should ring her at her hotel.

'Any special time?' My heart was racing, racing.

'Any time'll do. I'm not painting much. Just – thinking things over.'

'Very well, I'll be in touch.'

I took from my pocket the box of chocolates destined for Veronica, and gave them to her. She smiled again, said nothing. I thanked her for the lift, got out of the car. It trundled off down the snowy lane. The moon burnished its tiny roof. Its tyres left very narrow tracks in the snow. Neither of us waved.

In bed that night, frozen, shivering, wide awake, I began to think about the concept of romantic love. I had always been sceptical of its existence and was certainly innocent of its ways. Yet here I was, plainly seized by some extraordinary force, some unfamiliar form of madness, that made the rest of the night almost impossible to endure. I thought of the poets I loved – Shakespeare, Browning, Byron, Shelley – was this the sort of thing those chaps had been through? Was this the inspiration that had driven their genius? And to what measures would it drive me? My mind slithered, ineffectual as confused eels. Despite the cold, I was feverish, unable to lie still. Eventually, thank God, dawn paled the sky.

By mid-morning, I had established the nature of my brainstorm. It concerned love, and it was firing me with uncontainable restlessness. – The car, it seemed, was 'serious'. At least a week, they'd want it, with one man off, they said. I could not wait a week. I could not wait another moment.

Some instinct, though, forced me to endure two days. The weekend was the longest of my life. At last, on the Monday afternoon, in another snowstorm, I set off for The Black Swan with Ralphie. I had contemplated ringing Mary and asking her to come over in her car, but, after a thousand changes of mind, had decided that a surprise would be better. There were only two days left of my present leave. Already the weekend had been wasted, and Mary would be gone by the time I was back again.

Despite the deep snow, Ralphie and I made the seven miles to the hotel, across woods and fields, in less than an hour. A superhuman energy pressed me to keep up a wicked pace. By the time we arrived, I was sweating. Poor Ralphie was exhausted.

193

I saw Mary at once, through the glass door of the lounge. She was alone, reading a book by a small gas fire, a tiny glass of sherry on the table beside her.

'I've walked,' I said. 'The car won't be ready for a week. I couldn't – '

'Oh, Gerald,' she said. 'I thought you were never coming.' She looked abashed, as if she had not meant to say what she thought so quickly. 'But you're both frozen, soaked through!'

She patted Ralphie's head. At once the room, for all its emptiness, swirled with warmth and life, and I found myself sitting beside Mary in front of the pallid fire, shoes off, feet craning ungainly towards its pathetic heat, icy hands rasping together, speechless. As Mary seemed to be, too. At last, I said I was sorry I hadn't telephoned.

'I like surprises,' she said.

'Lunch?' I asked a while later. 'I'm ravenous.' This was a lie.

'Why not? Do you know, I'm the only guest here. God knows why they're open at this time of year. They say they have quite busy weekends, people coming to visit some home for disabled soldiers nearby. It'll be just us, and disgusting food.'

In the bleak, cold dining-room we ate the disgusting food and did not care: there was plenty of wine. An old woman with chilblained hands waited sullenly upon us, sniffing. Mary talked of her recent stay in Florence, and of her painting – 'not very good, but comforting' – and of her own labrador in Scotland, 'fatter than Ralphie'. Much of the time we ate in silence. There seemed no particular need for talk.

But come the castle pudding, with its smear of raspberry jam and skin-topped custard, and I could contain my curiosity no longer.

'Why are you here, exactly?' I asked.

Mary hesitated. I could see her working out an answer.

'Too complicated to explain, really,' she replied lightly. 'I'm just trying to work a few things out. I wanted to be somewhere a long way from home, by myself.'

'I see.' I would ask no more, naturally.

'I rather like being on my own. I really do,' she went on. 'In fact, if I never got married I'd be quite happy.' My mother would call that a terrible failure, but I honestly wouldn't mind at all.'

'I don't suppose there's much chance of your remaining . . .'

The vicious thought of her being someone else's wife stopped me. Mary gave a small laugh whose echo was muted by the mud-brown carpet, the soggy grey walls, the thick curtains of stuff like woven bran. By now it was three-thirty. Chilblains had left long ago in a huff. Mary offered me another lift home. But I insisted on walking. There was still energy to be dissipated if I was to get a wink of sleep that night.

'Very well, then,' she said. 'I'll drive over to *you* for lunch tomorrow. How would that be?'

That was the only moment she was just the slightest bit flirtatious. *My darling, beloved Mary – what do you imagine? And stay for ever, please.*

'Early as you like,' I said.

At midday I began to imagine that she was snowbound, upside down in a ditch, or had changed her mind. I suffered all the torments of a waiting lover, fretting over the smoky fire, the mud from Ralphie's paws on the sofa where she should sit, the draught from the windows. Provisions were a little odd, but by now I was confident she wouldn't mind that sort of thing. I had found one last bottle of port, given to me by my father on my twenty-first birthday, so pretty mature by now. Apart from that, there was a pound of sausages and a couple of stale rolls. The village shop had run out of pickles and cheese.

Mary arrived at one forty-five, by which time my equilibrium was in a wretched state. She had a shining cold face and wore green trousers: she gave no reason for being late.

'This,' she said, coming brilliantly into the room, a barren place, then, 'is *marvellous.*' She looked out of the window to the view I've lived with for forty years. 'Imagine when the apple tree is out.'

We grilled the sausages over the fire, burned and abandoned the rolls, and drank most of the port from my mother's old silver goblets. I put on the Beethoven violin concerto – scratchy old record, but it didn't matter. Nothing mattered. For the life of me, I can't remember what we talked about (the erosion of that conversation has been a mental torture ever since). But I

195

do remember we laughed a lot, made tea when it was dark and the wind fretted at the bare windows, and planned a walk together the next day – my last.

Each day with Mary, somehow, was so extraordinarily different, as if the Lord was giving us a chance, at least, to see each other in a variety of weathers. The Tuesday was sunny: great strips of gold slashed across the wind-bitten snow, draining the blue from shadows. Robins shrieked from the apple tree. The hedges, snow-covered chariots, were parked on cobweb wheels of diamond cogs, spun by millionaire spiders. Unable to stay indoors, I set off to the village with Ralphie, thinking I would meet her on her way. I sang 'Rule Britannia' very loudly, not knowing the words of any love songs, and found children skating on the pond. I thought: this is my last chance. What can I do? How can I let her go?

An immediate plan came to my rescue. For the first time in my honourable career, I would make some excuse and take two more days' leave. Thus, before she left, we might have a little more time.

I heard the pooping of a small horn behind me. The Austin Seven was chugging towards me, Mary in her woollen hat, smiling. She was out of the car in a trice, running.

'I'm terribly early. Sorry! Hope you didn't – I mean, we mustn't waste the sun.'

We didn't waste the sun. We walked for miles. God knows where we went. I remember woods, the creak of snow in the hush of ash trees, the squawk of a frightened blackbird. I remember a lighted village church, women bustling about with clumps of evergreen, preparing for a wedding or a funeral, a smell of paraffin, the organist perfecting 'Abide With Me'. Wickedly cold, suddenly, when we came out again. The sun had gone. The sky was a starless navy.

Mary was tired by now. We had had a glass of mulled wine in a pub, but had eaten nothing. Time ignored the ordinary junctions of an ordinary day. We were surprised by the suddenness of the evening. In a lane a mile still from the car, Mary suddenly slipped, stumbled. I put out my hand to save her, pulled her to me. Instead of resisting, she clung to me, a childlike hug with the fingers of her woolly gloves spread out on my arms. She gave a small sob. I could feel it against my heart. Looking down, I saw tears pushing under the long lashes of her closed eyes. I kissed her forehead. She straightened up, dabbed at her eyes. In the failing light, a smear of tears glinted on her cheek. I could see a drop of crystal poised under one nostril. We began to walk again. She let me hold her hand.

And, back at the car at last, she permitted me to kiss her on the forehead once more. In retrospect, I am glad, so glad, I was spared from knowing at the time this was our last moment. For, then, I had plans. Tomorrow I would surprise her: turn up in the mended car, take her to London, lunch, the Tate, theatre, dinner, anything. I said nothing of this, however, and shut the door of the toy-like car. She waved, this time, with a smile that I think was rather sad, but I may have imagined that. Working over the same small fabric of memory so many times, the weave plays tricks. Anyway, it was quite dark by now, and tonight no moon replaced the sun.

The following day I put on a suit and my regimental tie, polished my shoes. The Wolseley, full of new life, deposited me at The Black Swan at eleven-thirty precisely.

I asked for Miss Jay at the reception desk, as the lounge was empty. But she had gone. Checked out. No forwarding address. Nothing.

No need to remind myself of the pattern of my despair that followed, the struggle to heal a broken heart. I cursed myself for the stupid risk surprises mean, drove wildly to the Knights to make enquiries. They had left for Canada the day before. I skidded home to ring every Jay in the Borders' telephone book, but no one had heard of Mary. I wanted to end my life. I returned to being a soldier.

Six months later, almost to the day, I read in *The Times* the engagement was announced between Miss Mary Jay (address supplied, too late) to Mr Vaughan Robert Macdunnald of the Isle of Skye. (Oh God, had she waited six months for me to give some signal?) On one of Petronella's unwelcome visits, she mentioned that Mr Vaughan Macdunnald was a friend of her husband Henry, and the whole family would be going up to the wedding. Later, she tried to tell me about the nuptials. I told her that I had briefly met Mary Jay, but was not interested in hearing how her wedding day had passed. Petronella gave me one of her horribly knowing looks. I assumed, rightly, that I would have to avoid years of scraps of information pertaining to the Macdunnald household.

Three years after Mary's wedding, the Knights returned home. One evening I asked them, in a nonchalant manner, if they had ever heard of her again. They had not, though they had written to her at the time of her marriage. I went on, in casual fashion, to describe the nature of her departure.

'Well, it must have been very difficult for her, mustn't it?' said Janet. 'She'd come down here to try to persuade herself she couldn't go through with it, the marriage to Vaughan. But there was so much pressure on her. They had known each other since childhood, and he'd been trying to marry her for years, you know. Apparently he had a wonderful castle on the sea – everything you could want, if you loved Scotland, which Mary did. But he was blown up in '42 – helpless invalid for life. I think Mary believed that if she said no, that would be the end, for him.'

In the event, the end took forty years. Poor bugger. Poor Mary.

Mrs Cluff, I see, is coming up the garden path, basket over her arm, mind on the pork chop and baked apple she will cook for my lunch. She's a good soul, Mrs Cluff. And over those years, what for me? The odd fling, the casual affair, no thoughts of marriage: the saving discipline of army life, the pleasure of retirement here. I can't complain.

But, ah, what might have been? Should any old man ask himself that question? What might have been, with Mary Jay?

'Morning, General.' Doors bang. She's inclined to bang doors, Mrs Cluff.

'Morning, Mrs Cluff,' I shout back. We never come face to face until the dishes are on the table.

'Chill wind this morning.' Another bang.

And now she's free, my Mary Jay, and here am I still

waiting. Still waiting, in the real sense? Has the hope never died? Is the love of my life still intact in my heart? What do you think, Jacob old boy? Would I be a fool to risk getting in touch again, now – or a fool not to? Is it too late? Are we too old?

The morning has flown in cogitation. Damn sight more interesting, as a matter of fact, all that sort of thing, than the military side. Daresay Petronella and Co would be fascinated. But they'll never know, because it's not for publication, of course. Nothing private for publication.

I've taken my time balancing up the pros and cons, though the summing up needs another hour or so's reflection. Wind on the Common'll clear my mind. Then I'll make the decision, 'snappy', like my wise old CO said. By this evening, I promise myself. By 1800 hours, to be precise. Cheap dialling time. Quiet time to write a letter.

'Jacob,' I say, giving him a slight kick to wake him, 'Jacob, old man, it's an important day for you and me today. Come on, now. Stir yourself. It's almost time for lunch.'

Newport Borough Libraries